JV Fiction
j Staniszew
Staniszewski,
9001081760

W9-CBZ-724

My SORT OF Fairy Tale Ending

ANNA STANISZEWSKI

DISCARDED BY
MEAD PUBLIC LIBRARY

sourcebooks
jabberwocky

Copyright © 2013 by Anna Staniszewski
Cover and internal design © 2013 by Sourcebooks, Inc.
Cover design by Jennifer Jackman
Cover images by © Yuri Arcurs/Shutterstock, © Elenamiv/Shutterstock,
© Paul Almasy/CORBIS

Sourcebooks and the colophon are registered trademarks of Sourcebooks, Inc.

All rights reserved. No part of this book may be reproduced in any form or by
any electronic or mechanical means including information storage and retrieval
systems—except in the case of brief quotations embodied in critical articles or
reviews—without permission in writing from its publisher, Sourcebooks, Inc.

The characters and events portrayed in this book are fictitious or are used ficti-
tiously. Any similarity to real persons, living or dead, is purely coincidental and
not intended by the author.

Published by Jabberwocky, an imprint of Sourcebooks, Inc.
P.O. Box 4410, Naperville, Illinois 60567-4410
(630) 961-3900
Fax: (630) 961-2168
www.jabberwockykids.com

Library of Congress Cataloging-in-Publication data is on file with the publisher.

Source of Production: Versa Press, East Peoria, Illinois, USA
Date of Production: September 2013
Run Number: 21296

Printed and bound in the United States of America.
VP 10 9 8 7 6 5 4 3 2 1

9001081760

This book belongs to*:

_____

*Disclaimer: By printing your name above, you hereby agree to become an adventurer for life and vow to help all creatures of the magical variety (no matter how annoying they are).** Failure to carry out your duties will result in a disciplinary hearing before the Committee. Trust me; those old crones *will* make you cry.

We are not responsible for injuries sustained on missions. Avoid chomping goblins, stabbing leprechauns, creepy fairies, and other unpleasant creatures.*

***And by "unpleasant," we mean crazy and possibly fatal.

"There is no real ending. It's just the place where you stop the story."

—Frank Herbert

PART I

Chapter One

What did people bring with them when they were about to zip off to a mysterious fairy land to rescue their parents? I had no idea, but I figured I should at least pack a toothbrush. That way, if the fairies decided to torture me with magic dust or something, I'd at least have fresh, minty breath.

"Almost ready, Jenny?" Dr. Bradley asked from his perch by my desk. My magical mentor looked totally out of place sitting next to the piles of homework I'd be neglecting for however long this mission would take.

"I guess." Even though adventurers weren't supposed to get nervous, I was shaking all the way to my toes. What if I couldn't find my mom and dad? What if they weren't even in Fairy Land? What if this plan turned out to be one huge mistake?

Stop it, I told myself. Then I zipped up my backpack and threw it over my shoulder.

I could hear Aunt Evie downstairs, whistling along with one of her parakeet patients. Part of me wanted to go hug my aunt good-bye one more time, just in case, but I didn't want her to worry. Besides, I *would* see her again. I just knew it.

Pop! Anthony the Gnome materialized in the middle of my bedroom. For some reason, my magical guide was dressed in layers of climbing gear.

"Hey there, Jenny-girl!" he said, his harnesses and ropes rattling. He adjusted his headlamp, which barely fit over his mess of flame-colored hair. "Time to go!"

"Am I missing something?" I said. "Is Fairy Land in a big cave?"

Anthony shrugged. "If we're going to get your parents back, we need to be prepared for anything." He clapped his pudgy hands. "Okey dokey. Let's get going!"

Dr. Bradley grabbed his cane and hobbled over to us. Then the three of us clustered together, preparing for the awfulness of spinning in between worlds. I took a deep breath and—*Pop!*—we were sucked out of my bedroom, tossed around in a rainbow void, and spewed out onto...

My bedroom carpet?

Yup. We'd been spit out right back where we started.

"What happened?" I asked.

Dr. Bradley frowned and adjusted his small glasses. "I was afraid this might occur. Fairy Land has been closed off from the rest of the magical worlds for years. It's possible they have blocked our attempt to transport ourselves there."

"No problem-o!" said Anthony. "We'll try again."

"But if they're blocking us," I said, "then how will we—?"

"We just wear them down. That's what I always do in these situations."

Anthony certainly *was* good at wearing on people. Still, I couldn't help giving his shoulder an affectionate squeeze. He and Dr. Bradley knew how dangerous this mission might be. In fact, they'd even gone against the Committee—aka their annoying magical bosses—to help me. I usually tackled missions by myself, but this time I was glad to have help.

As Anthony grabbed my arm again, I closed my eyes and got ready for more inter-world spinning. *Pop!* I felt the carpet under my feet disappear. Then we swirled around and around like dizzy snowflakes.

Finally, my feet were on solid ground again. I opened my eyes.

We'd left my bedroom behind and were now in a fancy

chamber furnished in gold and red velvet. Weirdly, everything in the room was upside down. We were standing on the ceiling, looking down (or maybe up?) at the furniture. It was totally confusing.

"Oops," said Anthony. He took my hand again and—*Pop!*

More spinning through the void. I was starting to feel like an ice cube in a blender. We bounced in and out of world after world after world:

A concrete parking lot that stretched on forever.

A crystal lake with squirrels zipping around on miniature Jet Skis.

An empty landscape with a giant banana.

An empty landscape with two giant bananas.

An empty landscape with *no* bananas.

And the set of a TV sitcom.

"Anthony, stop!" I finally cried, feeling seriously sick to my stomach.

We materialized in a grassy field dotted with enormous wild turkeys. As Anthony let go of my hand, I realized the creatures weren't exactly turkeys. Their bodies were human-like, but they had droopy wings on their backs, and their oversized heads and necks were beakish and saggy. Gross.

"This is ridiculous," I said, my head throbbing. "We'll never get there at this rate."

The turkeys froze at the sound of my voice. Then their black eyes swung toward us. Their huge beaks opened, revealing flat, square teeth. Perfect for gobbling us up.

"Intruuuuders!" one of the turkey-monsters shrieked, flapping its scraggly wings.

"Get together!" Dr. Bradley cried as the turkeys started charging toward us.

Their beaks were only inches away when—*Pop!*—we disappeared into the void. I'd never felt so relieved to be sucked in between worlds.

"What were those things?" I said. My voice echoed for what felt like forever as colors swirled around us in a nauseating pattern.

"They were goblins," said Dr. Bradley.

Goblins? Since when were goblins giant turkey creatures? Then again, if there was one thing I'd learned during my three years as an adventurer, it was that magical creatures were actually nothing like they were in books and movies.

Thud! We landed on cold, hard ground. This time, we were in the middle of an old courtyard. The stones around us were crooked and mossy and dotted with tufts of yellow grass. I was relieved not to see any killer birds nearby.

"Where are we?" I said with a groan. I felt like someone had plucked off my arms and legs and reattached them upside down. I wasn't sure how much more world-jumping I could take.

Anthony let out a little squeal and pointed to a faded sign in the distance. "Welcome to Fairy Land," it said. "The Place of the Future."

"Fairy Land," I whispered. I had no idea what all that "future" stuff meant, but I didn't care. What mattered was that we'd finally made it! We were here!

I forgot all about my aching limbs and started to run toward the sign, grinning like a crazed monkey. Underneath it were rows of ticket booths, the kind you'd see at an entrance to an amusement park, and in the distance I spotted a crumbling roller coaster. I'd always thought "Fairy Land" sounded like the name of a theme park. It clearly used to be one, though it didn't look like anyone had used it in years.

I turned to ask Anthony about it, when—

Pop! Pop! Pop! Pop! Pop!

A blur of small figures appeared all around us, locking us in a tight circle.

My Sort of Fairy Tale Ending

"Don't move!" someone said. I couldn't see who it was. All I could see was the razor-sharp spear pointed right at my head.

Chapter Two

"Why have you come to Fairy Land?" a voice said.

When I was finally able to look past the spear, I realized the small figure at the other end of it was a leprechaun. He looked straight out of a cereal commercial: long beard, buckled shoes, and a shamrock attached to his green hat. Of course, I couldn't remember the last time I'd seen a leprechaun in a cereal commercial threatening someone with a deadly weapon.

I glanced at Dr. Bradley and Anthony who were huddled beside me, their arms raised in surrender. So much for the three of us going on our first adventure together.

"Don't mind us," Dr. Bradley piped up. "We were just passing through on our way to…" He trailed off, looking around at the overgrown fields and run-down amusement-park rides. The truth was that Fairy Land wasn't on the way to anywhere, except maybe that never-ending parking lot we'd accidentally popped into.

"Hey, no need to get all stabby," said Anthony, pushing one of the gleaming spears away from his neck. He never noticed when his life—or anyone else's—was in danger. "We just want to have a little chat with your queen."

Another guard stepped forward. He was shorter than the other leprechauns, but his dark beard was streaked with silver. He was twirling a shamrock between his lips like a farmer would do with a piece of straw. I could tell by the way the rest of the guards stood up straighter around him that he was the leader.

"No one can see the Queen Fairy," he said, his voice surprisingly low for someone barely half my height. "Now please gold."

"Um, do you mean *go?*" I said.

"Gold," the leprechaun insisted. He stretched out his arm and pointed his finger in the universal gesture for "scram."

Not a chance. We'd come all this way to follow up on the only lead we had about where my parents might have gone, and I wasn't "golding" anywhere until I knew for sure they weren't in Fairy Land.

"Why can't we see the queen?" I asked. "Is she invisible or something?"

"No one is allowed to insult the Queen Fairy," the head guard said, practically shoving his spear up my nostril.

"Whoa!" I held my hands up way over my head. I hadn't come to Fairy Land to get an unwanted nose piercing. "I'm not insulting anyone. I was just wondering why we can't see her."

"Hey," Anthony chimed in. "Stop waving that pointy stick around!"

The head guard's eyes narrowed. "Enough." He motioned with his hand, as if he was about to do some serious magic on us. But nothing magical happened; instead, a loud buzzing sound erupted from a red cuff around the leprechaun's wrist.

The other leprechauns looked away in embarrassment, like they'd accidentally seen the head guard in his underwear.

"What's going on?" I said, pointing at the cuff. "Why is it making that sound?"

"Nothing to worry about," he mumbled, his round cheeks turning pink. "I just went over my magic ration for the day, that's all."

Wait. Were the leprechauns on magical diets or something? *Join Wand Watchers today and watch the magical pounds melt away!*

I glanced over at Dr. Bradley just in time to see him wink at me. Hopefully, that meant he had something up his sleeve that would get us out of this mess.

The head guard gave his bracelet a fierce twist, and it finally stopped buzzing. Just then another loud sound echoed around us. *Pop!*

Dr. Bradley vanished.

The leprechauns stopped trying to stab us and charged toward the spot where the doctor had been. Seeing my chance, I grabbed Anthony's hand and ran as fast as I could through the knee-high grass toward a cluster of nearby rides.

"Stop!" one of the leprechauns called after us.

Then a heavy orange cuff that looked a lot like the red ones the leprechauns wore appeared on my wrist. Anthony had an identical one around his wrist too. It perfectly matched his hair. I had no idea what the cuffs were for.

"Anthony, get us out of here," I cried as I dragged him past a crumbling spaceship ride.

"All right. All right," he said, huffing. His short gnome legs weren't really designed for running, and all the harnesses and ropes he'd draped on himself weren't helping. The gnome snapped his fingers…but nothing happened.

"What's the matter?" I said.

"I don't know." He kept snapping his fingers, but it still wasn't working. "Maybe the cuff did something to my magic."

Great. I glanced over my shoulder and spotted the dozen leprechauns sprinting after us. We had to find somewhere to hide.

In any other kingdom, Anthony would've known his way around and been able to give me directions. But since Fairy Land had been cut off from the rest of the magical worlds for years, we were pretty much running around in a black hole.

"Head for that Ferris wheel!" I said. It wasn't a great hiding spot, but our only other option was a teacup ride. There was no way the leprechauns would mistake us for lumps of sugar.

We sped up, trying to lose the leprechauns in the tall grass. They were so short that they could barely see over it. Just when I was starting to think we might lose the guards, Anthony tripped over his climbing harnesses and sailed to the ground.

"Take that stuff off!" I cried, pulling him to his feet.

Anthony scrunched his face up in annoyance, but he

tore off his gear and cast it aside. "Don't blame me if we get stuck somewhere with no way to climb out," he said.

Finally, we got to the ancient Ferris wheel. It was rusted and sagging and clearly hadn't been used in years. We ducked behind a dented control panel and tried to catch our breath. I hadn't noticed it before, but the buckets of the Ferris wheel were shaped like flying saucers. In fact, most of the rides we'd passed had been space-related. Maybe that's what the "Place of the Future" stuff on the welcome sign had been all about.

"I think we're safe," Anthony wheezed. He grabbed one of the Ferris-wheel seats to steady himself.

"No, don't!" I said, but it was too late.

CREEEEEEAK!

Slowly, the Ferris wheel started to turn, making the loudest, most horrible sound I'd ever heard. Anthony jumped away from it with his hands up, as if he'd had nothing to do with revealing our hiding spot.

Pop! Pop! Pop! Pop! Pop!

The leprechauns materialized all around us. The head guard might have run out of magic, but the others had plenty to go around.

"Freeze!" they cried.

Chapter Three

"Look," I said to the leprechauns, "can't we all just get along? Let's sit down and talk about this." Wow, it was rare that two cheesy sayings popped out of my mouth at once. I guess that meant I was feeling pretty desperate.

The head guard let go of one of the other leprechaun's elbows and stepped forward. Clearly, he'd hitched a magical ride in order to follow us.

"I'm afraid not," he said, still sucking on a shamrock stem. "If you refuse to leave this land, then you must gold with us."

A guard grabbed my backpack while another took away the pouch of medicines Anthony always wore around his waist.

"Hey! Give those back!" I said, but no one was listening to me.

"Fabulous," Anthony muttered as the leprechauns

pulled his arms behind his back. "The doctor made a run for it, and now we're stuck here."

"He didn't make a run for it," I whispered. "He was trying to distract the guards so we could get away and look for my parents." Too bad that plan had completely failed. I glanced around, wondering if Dr. Bradley was hiding somewhere nearby, but there was no sign of him.

"Now, for the last time," said the head guard, coming to stand right in front of me. "Who are you, and what do you want?"

I sighed. "I'm Jenny the Adventurer, and I'm just here looking for my—"

"An adventurer?" the leprechaun said, stepping back in surprise. "Are you really an adventurer?"

"Um…" Technically I guess I wasn't, not anymore. Not since the Committee had refused to do anything about finding my parents, giving me no choice but to defy orders and go to Fairy Land to find them on my own. But the fact that the guards were suddenly looking at me differently made me decide not to 'fess up about having gone rogue.

"Yes, I am *an adventurer*. And last I checked, the Committee wasn't a big fan of its employees being attacked. So how about taking it easy with those weapons?"

The leprechauns glanced at each other. Then the head guard gave a signal, and they all lowered their spears and took a step back.

"My apologies," he said with a small bow. "I am Karfum, head of the Leprechaun Guard. Please, forgive our rudeness. Of course, we will bring you to the palace." He pointed to a village in the distance that I hadn't noticed before (probably because I'd been too busy running for my life). It was covered in a cloud of glittering haze.

Anthony and I glanced at each other. What was going on? Why did knowing I was an adventurer change the leprechauns' minds about us?

Karfum signaled to the other leprechauns, who turned and fell into a single line. "Please, after you," he said, waving us forward.

"Wait," I said. "Before we gold—um, I mean, go— anywhere, how about taking these cuffs off us? And giving us our stuff back?"

Karfum gave a regretful shake of his head. "The Queen Fairy insists that all residents, even honored guests such as yourselves, wear the cuffs for security reasons. Your belongings will be returned to you when you leave this land."

I gawked at the guard. The leprechauns had been ready

to Swiss-cheese us with their spears a minute ago, and now we were honored guests? Fairy Land was getting weirder by the second, and we hadn't even seen a fairy yet.

"What do you think?" I asked Anthony in a low voice. "Should we go with him?"

Anthony shrugged. "Until we figure out how to get these cuffs off, I guess we don't have a choice."

He was right. This wasn't how I'd wanted to go about rescuing my parents, but I was willing to do whatever it took to get them back. I would *not* go home empty-handed again.

"Fine," I said to the guard. "Lead the way."

As we followed the leprechauns, my fingers instinctively went to the string of purple gems around my neck that had once been my mother's. I'd only just managed to get the necklace back from an evil witch a few days earlier—along with the tip about my parents' whereabouts—but already it felt like it had always sat around my neck.

If my mom and dad aren't here, a small voice in the back of my brain whispered, *what will I do then?*

Quiet, I told the voice. *My parents have to be in Fairy Land. Because if they're not…*

I pictured going back home without them. Living in

Aunt Evie's animal-filled house for the rest of my life, always wondering what had happened to my mom and dad. Always hoping they'd magically appear someday. Always feeling like a big part of my life was missing. I couldn't imagine a more depressing future.

As I glanced toward the heart of Fairy Land, I promised myself that I wouldn't let that future happen. My parents had to be here. And I would do anything—anything at all—to get them back.

I mean, come on. I'd helped dozens of creatures get their happy endings. Hadn't I earned my own happily-ever-after?

* * *

As we got closer to the village, the overgrown fields became freshly paved roads and neat rows of identical, red-roofed huts. The haze that I'd seen from a distance was now all around us. It gave everything the type of weird glow that people have in wrinkle-cream commercials.

"I don't get it. I thought this place was a futuristic theme park," I said to Anthony.

The gnome shrugged. "I guess things have changed now that the King Fairy isn't in power. I hope they at least have cotton candy."

It figured that even when we'd been taken prisoner, all Anthony could think about was food.

Just then, we heard rumbling coming toward us. As the guards waved us off the road, a carriage rounded the corner. It was shaped like a pumpkin and pulled by a team of white horses. The whole thing was straight out of *Cinderella*. A second later, another identical carriage passed by. And then a third. All of them were empty.

"What are those all about?" I said.

"They're taxis," said Karfum. He pointed ahead. "We are nearly at the palace now."

Through the glittery haze, I could just make out a building that looked a lot like Cinderella's castle. In fact, everything about this place screamed Disney. It was starting to creep me out.

Suddenly, a loud *Bing!* echoed around us. The leprechauns froze and tipped their heads upward.

"*Just a reminder*," a cheerful voice rang out from somewhere above us. "*The weekly parade is only a few days away! Attendance is mandatory. Remember that all work and no play makes for a dull fairy!*"

I groaned. That was even cheesier than the sayings I was always spouting during adventures.

"A parade!" said Anthony, his eyes gleaming with excitement. "Do you think we can go? I bet they'll be selling candied applies and fried dough and—"

"Sorry, we won't be here by then," I said, hoping that was true.

"Come along," said Karfum as the guards started moving again. Now that they knew I was an adventurer, they seemed to want to get me to the palace as fast as possible. Either they were afraid I'd try to run off again, or they didn't want me to spoil before the fairies got a chance to gobble me up.

We passed by a sign over the entrance to a narrow alleyway that said: "Welcome to the Magical Village." Behind it were clusters of cute little shops that looked like they should be bursting with elves making shoes.

Anthony gasped beside me.

I turned to see a huge, purple ogre blocking our way. He didn't look like he had any intention of letting us pass.

Chapter Four

Anthony jumped behind me, using me as a shield. Ever since an ogre had tried to chew off his toes a few months ago, my guide had been a little nervous around all ogre types.

This one was different from other ogres I'd seen, not just because of his rough purple skin, but also because of the single eye and horn on his head, and the pointed wings on his back.

Wait. One-eyed, one-horned, flying, and purple? No way. I was looking at a purple people eater! Too bad my best friends Trish and Melissa were still in the Land of Tales. They would be so jealous when I told them about this—Trish because she loved meeting unusual creatures and Melissa because she loved singing the purple people eater song.

"What are you doing outside, Pryll?" Karfum called. "It's the middle of the workday."

"I came to deliver a warning," the creature said, lumbering toward us. "Tell the fairies this is their last chance."

Karfum's lips became a thin line, and I was afraid he'd accidentally swallow his shamrock. "Pryll, you're putting everyone, including my son, in danger. It's best if you—"

"No!" said the creature, stomping his purple foot. "We have waited long enough. Will you deliver the message or not?"

Karfum sighed and nodded. "I will."

"What message?" I interrupted, stepping forward. The monster glared at me with his one eye. "Um, Mr. People Eater, sir?" I added.

"You're new arrivals, eh?" said Pryll with a shake of his head that sent his single eye spinning like a police siren. "She won't let you leave, you know. We thought once the park was closed, she'd let all of us workers go back to our worlds. But we'll make her pay. Just you watch." He kept grumbling to himself as he shuffled away, his wings bouncing, and disappeared down one of the narrow streets.

"What was that all about?" I said as Anthony emerged from cowering behind a couple of guards.

"I am not at liberty to say," Karfum answered. He looked suddenly nervous as he popped a handful of shamrocks into his mouth and started chewing on them. When he saw me staring, he mumbled: "Shamrocks are great for everything, even stress."

Normally, I would have laughed at the idea of shamrocks being a wonder drug, but I was too busy replaying what Pryll had said about no one ever leaving this place. Anthony must have been thinking the same thing because he leaned over and whispered: "No wonder so many adventurers have disappeared here."

"Wait, *what?*" I cried before managing to lower my voice. "I thought my parents were the only adventurers who were missing. Are you saying others have vanished too?"

Anthony nodded. "At first the Committee thought they'd just gotten sick of their jobs, but now it looks like they were brought to Fairy Land. Just like your parents were."

"And when were you planning on telling me about this?" If other adventurers had disappeared, that could be a big clue about what the fairies were doing to my parents.

"I just did, didn't I?"

Anthony must have seen the steam coming out of my ears because he quickly changed the subject by turning to Karfum and saying, "So, I had no idea leprechauns worked for the fairies. I thought you all pretty much kept to yourselves."

A few of the guards around us stiffened.

"We leprechauns cannot gold back to our land," said Karfum. He'd swallowed his mouthful of shamrocks and was back to sucking on just one stem again.

"What do you mean?" I said. "All of you? The entire leprechaun population?"

"Yes," a female guard said. I could tell she was a woman because her face was a little softer and her beard a little thinner than that of the other leprechauns. Not surprisingly, she was wearing shamrocks as earrings. "We must remain here until we have our pots of gold back."

It took me a second to realize she actually meant "gold" this time. "Why, what happened to them?" I asked.

No one answered. Either they didn't know or they didn't want to talk about it. I imagined an abandoned leprechaun world, just sitting there like a giant frowny face. How depressing.

When we got to the entrance of the palace, the tallest of the guards stepped forward. "Tickets, please!" he called. The others immediately took out green slips of paper and handed them over before filing into the palace.

"Tickets?" the tall leprechaun said when Anthony and I got to the front of the line. "You need tickets to gold on from this point."

Anthony pulled a couple of candy wrappers from his pocket and tried to hand them over, but the leprechaun just sniffed and shook his head.

"Why would we have tickets?" I said. "You guys captured us, remember?"

Karfum stepped in. "I believe we can make an exception."

The tall leprechaun sighed and thrust two slips of paper into our hands. "Tickets?" he said cheerfully. He took the pieces of paper right back and handed them over to one of the other guards, who stuck them in his pocket.

Fairy Land was obviously having a hard time shaking its theme-park roots.

We went through the enormous palace doors and into a hallway with cathedral ceilings and gilded walls. Your typical fairy-tale castle. Then we rounded a corner and found ourselves in front of an elevator.

"An elevator?" I said. "Doesn't that seem a little out of place?"

Karfum shrugged. "It's one of the few features the Queen Fairy allowed to remain from when this land was a theme park."

"Why do you need elevators?" said Anthony. "Can't you just pop yourselves wherever you want to go?" He was still puffing from our long walk to the palace. I'm sure he would have preferred to be magically transported here rather than having to trudge all that way.

"No," the lady leprechaun said as she held up her red cuff. "We are required to conserve our magic whenever possible."

As we got into the elevator, I could actually feel the magic all around us, like nonstop static electricity. I thought of the people in the Land of Tales whose power had been stolen by the Queen Fairy. They would kill to have even an ounce of that magic back. What did the queen want with it all?

The minute the elevator started moving, all the leprechauns raised their arms straight up in the air and screamed as if they were on a roller coaster. "Ahhhh!"

Anthony clapped his hands over his ears and leaped into my arms like a terrified cat.

"Stop that!" I yelled at the guards, but the leprechauns kept on screaming right until the elevator stopped.

"What's with all the shrieking?" Anthony demanded as the door slid open and he jumped out of my arms.

Karfum shrugged like there was nothing weird about it. "That is the protocol here."

28

I had to laugh. "You mean you're supposed to scream every time you go up the elevator?"

"And down," said the female guard. "It took us some time to get used to it, but now we barely notice it anymore. The fairies all do it. You'll see."

I didn't want to see. I wanted to find my parents and get as far away from this crazy place as possible.

We left the elevator and walked into an elaborate ballroom. Yet another thing that looked totally Disney. I could almost imagine dancing teapots flitting by. If any princes started singing at me, things would get ugly really fast.

As we shuffled into the room, I spotted a tall, thin woman in a poufy blue dress and even poufier gray hair gliding toward us. The closer she got, the taller she looked and the narrower her face appeared. When she was in front of us, I had to swallow a gasp. This creature didn't look anything like a fairy, no shimmery wings in sight. In fact, she looked like an alien, the outer space kind—pale skin, catlike eyes, and gangly limbs—if that alien was dressed up like Cinderella's fairy godmother.

I expected her to cry "Bibbity-bobbity-boo" and start singing, but instead she said, "Greetings," in a low voice that didn't fit her I-just-stepped-out-of-a-UFO looks. "I am Lady Mahlia, the Queen Fairy's assistant. And you are Jenny the Adventurer. We have been waiting for you."

Chapter Five

"What do you mean, you've been waiting for me?" I said.

Mahlia's lips stretched into a fake smile that reminded me of the sewn-on grins you see on mascots. I couldn't get over her outfit. Aliens weren't supposed to dress up like Disney characters. And they definitely weren't supposed to have white powder in their hair to make it look gray. Had she just come from acting in a school play or something?

"We knew that Ilda's information would lead you here eventually," Mahlia said, waving around a star-shaped wand, just like a fairy godmother was supposed to have.

So the witch *had* been telling the truth—at least about the fairies being involved in my parents' disappearance. It figured that alienlike creatures would be all about abducting people.

"Unfortunately," Mahlia went on, her painful smile fading, "she misled you. We had nothing to do with your parents disappearing." She stepped forward. "We are so thrilled you came to us. We love adventurers."

I couldn't help taking a step back as I noticed a weird, hungry look on her face. Did she mean they liked to *eat* adventurers?

"Hey there," Anthony said, stepping forward. He never liked being left out of things. "I'm Anthony, Jenny's guide."

Mahlia gave him a weak smile and turned back to me. "I am sure you have many questions about our kingdom, but first—"

"Where's Ilda?" I interrupted. "Is she here?"

"She is our honored guest. We have encouraged her to stay with us until it is safe for her to return to her land."

Yeah, right. They probably had her in a dungeon or something. The fairies couldn't have been happy about the witch spilling the Queen Fairy's secrets to me.

"You sure have a lot of honored guests around here," I said.

"We thrive on visitors. We have for decades." Mahlia gestured out the window at the hazy village below, as if it were teeming with life. But the streets were totally empty, like a beach in the winter.

"That's not what I heard," Anthony muttered. "Ever

since the king died, you guys have had a reputation for being pretty darn unfriendly. I mean…a theme park without an ounce of cotton candy?"

"We are *not* a theme park," Mahlia said through a tight smile. "The Queen Fairy put a stop to that foolishness long ago. She saved us and helped rebuild our land so that we could embrace our true fairy nature." She waved her wand around again, like she was trying to act the part of a stereotypical fairy. It made her look like she was conducting an orchestra that only she could see.

"If you say so," said Anthony.

Okay, enough small talk. "We need to see the Queen Fairy," I said. According to Ilda, the queen was the one who'd arranged to have my parents kidnapped. There was no way I was leaving this place without talking to her.

Mahlia shook her head. "I am afraid that is impossible. But our land has so much to offer! How about I set up a tour for you and your friend?"

"We don't want a tour. We just—"

"Our castle is exquisite! And the queen will be holding a ball tomorrow for—"

"A ball?" I jumped in. "Will she be there?"

The fairy let out a tinkling laugh. "I am afraid not,

but there will be plenty of other delightful fairies to mingle with."

"I don't want to mingle! All I want is to see the queen. I'm not going anywhere until you let me talk to her!"

Mahlia blinked at me. I realized I'd been yelling right in her face. But what did she expect? I wasn't going to just give up on finding my parents when it felt like I was so close.

"Very well," Mahlia said, her smile dimming. "I will try to arrange an audience with the queen. Be warned, she will likely say no. She is very private."

Right, private. Or an adventurer-eating monster who'd slurp up my brain while I slept.

"In the meantime," Mahlia went on, her face brightening, "please make yourselves at home in our wonderful land." As she waved her wand again, I noticed a red cuff around her wrist, just like the ones the leprechauns wore. Did that mean she was on a magical diet too?

"Pardon me, Lady Mahlia," said Karfum. He stepped forward and whispered into one of the fairy's long ears. I could make out the words "Pryll" and "threat."

As the fairy listened intently, she not so subtly scratched her powdered hair with one of the points of her wand. When Karfum was done talking, Mahlia gave us a little bow of her head and said, "My apologies. I have an urgent matter to attend to. The guards will show you to your rooms." She turned and started to glide away.

Rooms? How long did they think we'd be staying here? "Wait!" I said. "We don't want to sleep here! Let us see the queen and then we'll go home."

Mahlia turned back to me and let out a twittering laugh. "Oh, Jenny. You will enjoy Fairy Land so much that you will never want to leave."

I shuddered. I could just imagine the fairies saying that exact same thing to my parents all those years ago, before they'd trapped them here forever.

Chapter Six

The leprechauns brought us down one endless corridor after another, until I started to get dizzy. I kept expecting to see other fairies, but there was no one around except for the occasional leprechaun who was cleaning, guarding, or doing some other super-boring task.

"This place is the worst," Anthony huffed, probably still miffed about being ignored because he wasn't an adventurer. Personally, I thought he was pretty lucky not to be on the fairies' radar.

"Where is everybody?" I asked Karfum as he led us down yet another hallway. "How come Mahlia is the only fairy we've seen?"

The leprechaun cleared his throat. "Everyone is currently working in the factories below."

Elevators and factories in a fairy-tale castle? Nothing about this place added up.

"Doing what?" said Anthony. His eyes lit up. "Making candy, by any chance?"

"I thought you were done with candy," I said.

Anthony shrugged. "Thanks to this mission, I won't be going to my high-school reunion anymore. Now I don't have to worry about indulging once in a while."

"Yes, there are food factories," the female leprechaun said, "and a variety of other industries. Now that the magic is rationed, everyone must work for their necessities."

"How long has the rationing been going on?" I asked. No one answered my question. Maybe it was yet another thing they weren't supposed to talk about. I couldn't figure it out. The leprechauns were servants, so it made sense not to give them too much power, but why were the fairies forced to limit their magic too? With all the magic the queen had stolen from other lands, surely there was more than enough to go around.

As we went through the palace, I kept an eye out for Dr. Bradley, but there was still no sign of him. Maybe he wasn't even in Fairy Land anymore. I wouldn't put it past him to go beg the Committee members to help us, but since they'd already told us they thought the whole mission was "imprudent," I doubted he'd have any luck.

We rounded another corner and almost smacked into a troll.

Anthony shrieked like a little girl and sputtered: "What—what…?"

I couldn't blame Anthony for being terrified. The troll wasn't just a troll. He was a troll in a troll costume. His oversized plush troll head was tucked under his arm while his real troll head was poking out of the top of his costume. It was totally disorienting.

"Remember the rules, Froy," said Karfum. "Heads must be worn at all times in public."

The troll sighed and plopped his fake head on top of his real one. Did the fairies think he wasn't "troll enough" so they'd put him in a costume? If this was another one of the Queen Fairy's ideas, then I was starting to think she was completely insane.

Finally, after making us wind through a few more hallways—were they leading us in circles?—the guards stopped at an oval-shaped door and turned to Anthony.

"This will be your room," said Karfum. "Since you have expressed a liking for candy, we'll make sure it is fully stocked with anything you desire."

Anthony's eyes tripled in size. "Any candy I want?" he said in a whisper.

The leprechaun nodded and ushered Anthony into the room. The gnome glanced over his shoulder at me. "I guess I'll see you later, Jenny-girl." Then the door closed, and he was gone.

"And these," Karfum said, leading me to an oval-shaped door across the hall as the other guards trailed behind us, "are your quarters."

When he opened the door, I actually gasped. The entire place was set up like a mini-golf course. There was even a water trap in the middle of the room that doubled as a fountain.

"How—how did you guys know I love mini-golf?" I said.

The leprechaun shrugged like it wasn't a big deal. I guess he was used to fairies knowing more than they should.

I glanced at the other guards still in the hallway, then lowered my voice. "So now what?" I asked Karfum. "You're just going to leave me here?" I had a feeling the door would lock from the outside the minute the guard left. "I need to see the queen. Please, it's really important." I couldn't believe it when tears started stinging at my eyes. Since when was I a crier? I guess getting so close to finding my parents only to feel like I was still a million miles away from them was getting to me.

Karfum sighed and handed me a green handkerchief which, weirdly, was made out of woven shamrocks. I dabbed at my eyes with it to be polite and then handed it back to him, hoping I didn't have some sort of allergic reaction to shamrock pollen.

"You are just like my daughter," he said, his voice soft and soothing. "She was always so impatient. Just wait a while. You never know what's waiting around the corner." His eyes got a far-off look that made me wonder what had happened to his daughter.

"Karfum," I said softly. "Please, tell me what's going on here. Do the fairies trap adventurers? Do they have my parents? Are they going to eat me?"

The softness in the leprechaun's face disappeared and was quickly replaced by the same emotionless mask he'd been wearing when I first met him. "I'm afraid those are things I'm not allowed to speak of."

Then he turned and left me alone in my amazing mini-golf room. I should have been in heaven, but all I wanted to do was scream.

Chapter Seven

After hitting a mini-golf ball under the bed and through the bathroom, I tried to hack at the front door of my room with the club. With the first thwack, an electriclike zap went down my arm. The door wasn't just locked; it was sealed with magic. The fairies could dress it up all they wanted, but I was a prisoner, plain and simple.

I hurried over to the window, hoping I could escape that way if I needed to, only to discover that it was made out of super-thick glass and also sealed shut with magic. Great.

Suddenly, I jumped as a knocking sound came from a nearby closet.

"Um, who's there?" I said.

"Me," a hushed voice answered.

"Me who?" Apparently, I was part of some weird knock-knock joke.

"Just open the door!"

I flung open the closet to find a fairy boy around my age crouched inside. When he climbed out, I saw he was taller than I was, and much ganglier thanks to his alienlike arms and legs. He was also wearing clothes that I would expect to see on a fairy-tale prince, not on a fairy—including red tights. Tights! At least his pale hair wasn't powdered white. And even with the weird getup, I had to admit that he was still kind of cute.

"Who are you?" he said, an accusing tone in his voice.

"I'm Jenny. Who are you?"

"I am Luken," the boy barked. "I live next door. What have you done with Belthum?"

"Who's Belthum?" I tried not to giggle as I kept staring at the boy's tights. Was this really how fairies dressed? Or was it all part of the Cinderella vibe in this place?

"The leprechaun who lives here. This is very important. I need to know where he is!" The fairy boy looked like he might start trying to shake the truth out of me. His intensity was a far cry from Mahlia's fake happiness.

"Hey, calm down. I have no clue where your leprechaun friend is. Or who he is. The guards just brought me here."

The boy shook his head and started pacing around the room, rubbing one of his pointy ears with his fingers. I noticed he had a red cuff around his wrist, just like the one Mahlia and the leprechauns wore. "This is not good," he muttered. "The Queen's Guard must have found out what we were planning."

"Planning what?" I said, but Luken didn't answer.

Finally, he let out a long sigh and glanced around at my personal mini-golf course. "They have customized the room for you. I suppose that means Belthum is really gone," he said. Then his eyes lit up. "Wait. You are the adventurer."

As he studied me curiously, there was none of the hunger I'd seen in Mahlia's face. Maybe that meant fairies didn't eat adventurers, after all. Not that I'd actually been worried. And even if they did try to wolf me down, I'd probably just taste like anger and impatience.

"Yup, that's me. Jenny the Adventurer," I said. "Now will you tell me why you're so upset? What do you think happened to your friend?"

Luken closed his catlike eyes for a second. Then he stepped forward and said in a low voice, like he thought someone else might be listening: "I am afraid he has been moused."

"Moused?" I repeated. I thought of the troll in a troll costume I'd seen walking around. Had Luken's leprechaun friend been forced to wear a Mickey Mouse costume or the Fairy Land equivalent? Judging by the pained look on Luken's face, I had a feeling it was something even worse.

Then he blinked a couple of times and jumped up with what looked like excitement. "An adventurer ride!" he said before pulling a sketch pad out of his back pocket.

"Um, what?" I asked as he started drawing furiously.

He ignored me and kept scribbling. When I glanced over his shoulder, I almost laughed when I saw a sketch of a roller coaster that was roughly shaped like my face.

"What on earth is that?" I said.

Luken's eyes snapped up, like he'd totally forgotten I was in the room. "Nothing," he said, his cheeks flushing pink. "Just an idea for a design. But it...it is not any good." He shoved the sketch pad back in his pocket.

Before I could ask him more about it, footsteps echoed out in the hallway.

Luken sprinted across the room and stopped at the closet opposite to the one he'd come through. Then he ducked inside and started looking for something.

"What are you doing?" I said.

"I must go search for Belthum before anyone notices I am missing. There is another trapdoor here. If I can just find the latch—ah! There it is." He turned back to me. "Good luck, Jenny the Adventurer."

"Wait!" I cried. "Where do the trapdoors go?" I could have kicked myself for not checking the closets when I first got here.

"Through all of the rooms along this side of the corridor," he said over his shoulder.

"Any chance one of them leads to the queen?"

Luken didn't answer. He'd already ducked into the closet and was climbing through the panel in back.

Without thinking, I dove in after him. The minute my head went through the panel, the orange cuff around my wrist let out a horrible buzzing sound and zapped me with electricity like a wonky toaster.

I fell backward onto the carpet of my room, just as the front door burst open. Karfum stood in the doorway with several other guards behind him.

"Did you miss me already?" I said with a forced laugh, checking to see if smoke was coming out of my mouth. Luckily, the cuff had only shocked me instead of frying my insides.

"You were trying to leave your room," said the female guard.

As I scrambled to my feet, I glanced over to make sure the trapdoor in the closet was totally hidden. There was no sign of Luken.

"What?" I said. "No, I wasn't! That's crazy! I would never do that." Okay, maybe I was denying it a little too much. I'd never been a great liar.

"Your tracker," said Karfum. "We know it—" He fell silent and stared off into space, as if he were listening to a far-off sound. Then he nodded slightly and said: "I have just received word that the queen has requested to see you immediately."

I stared at him. "So soon? But everyone's been saying the Queen Fairy never sees anyone."

"She has changed her mind. In fact, she was particularly interested to meet you once she discovered you were an adventurer."

I shuddered. What was it with fairies and adventurers?

"Now, we must hurry and get you ready," said Karfum. "If you do not look presentable, the queen will be displeased."

I stared in horror as the leprechauns conjured up piles of clothes and toiletries. Karfum and a few of the other guards went to wait out in the hallway, while two female leprechauns practically tied me down to a chair, promising that I'd love my makeover.

They tugged and painted and spritzed until I felt like my head had been turned into papier-mâché. Then the female guards dressed me up in a huge, sparkly gown that looked like something my aunt might have worn to her prom.

"Are you kidding?" I said. "I can't wear this!" I felt like a wedding cake on legs. At least I'd persuaded the leprechauns to let me keep my sneakers on, since they'd be hidden under the long dress, instead of having to wear the high-heeled torture devices they'd laid out for me.

When the guards finally let me see myself in the mirror, all I could do was stare. My hair was in curls—I didn't know my hair *could* curl—my eyes were about twice their usual size, and my lips looked (and tasted) like candy. As tacky as the dress was, its layers of sparkly netting were actually flattering on me. I had to admit that I looked kind of…pretty.

"Perfect," said one of the leprechauns in her deep voice. "The queen will approve." Then she pushed me out into the hall.

Chapter Eight

When the elevator opened onto the very top floor of the palace, Karfum and the other guards stepped back, leaving me standing alone in the entryway. I'd barely even heard them screaming on the trip up. I couldn't stop thinking about all the things I was going to say to the Queen Fairy, including how much I hated her for tearing my family apart.

A loud *Bing!* rang out in the elevator. Another fake-chipper announcement.

"*Just a reminder!*" the voice said. "*It is now the end of the workday. All workers are required to go home, relax, and put their feet up!*"

Hmm. Nothing like forced relaxation to make you feel totally stressed out.

"Gold ahead," Karfum told me after the announcement had ended.

"Aren't you going to collect a ticket or something?" Okay, maybe I was stalling a little bit. The truth was, after all this time of desperately trying to see the queen, I wasn't sure I was ready to face her. After all, she was my last hope of getting my parents back.

"Gold," Karfum said again. "The Queen Fairy is waiting for you."

I took a deep breath and stepped out into the hallway as the elevator door shut behind me. Then I wound through a maze of candlelit stone corridors. I had to kick my dress out of the way as I walked so it wouldn't trip me. Maybe the queen liked everyone to dress this way so they'd have a hard time running away.

Stationed throughout the corridor were beefy fairies dressed in military-style uniforms and armed with everything from spears to bows to swords. This had to be the Queen's Guard that Luken had told me about. I guess the queen only trusted fellow fairies to be her personal bodyguards. The fairies didn't even look at me as I passed, but I had a feeling that if I were an intruder, they'd slice and dice me in less than a second.

Finally, the hallway opened onto a huge room with a domed ceiling that reminded me of a planetarium. Maybe back when this land had been a futuristic theme park, this room had been used for viewing stars. Now it reminded me of the throne room from the cartoon version of *Cinderella*.

As I moved farther into the room, the pale stone walls started to flicker with colors. I couldn't believe it. They were actually *showing* the cartoon version of *Cinderella*.

Seriously. What was wrong with this place?

I jumped as a high-pitched voice piped in from my left: "Welcome, Jenny the Adventurer." Then a figure emerged from behind a hanging tapestry.

My breath stuck in my throat.

Before me stood a fairy and yet not a fairy. She was more like a glowing fairy-shaped creature in a huge, silvery-blue gown. Sure enough, the dress was straight out of *Cinderella*. Clearly, someone was a fan.

Strangely, the Queen Fairy's skin wasn't pale like that of the other fairies. Instead, it gleamed golden as if sunlight were oozing out of her pores. I actually had to squint to look at her.

I couldn't help thinking of an old movie that Aunt Evie and I had watched about glowing aliens that could float through the air. The fact that the fairies matched so many alien clichés couldn't be a coincidence, right? They could get rid of their UFO theme park, but I certainly wasn't fooled.

"Please curtsy," said the Queen Fairy.

I obeyed without even thinking about it, grabbing the edges of my dress and bobbing up and down. The queen's presence was just that powerful.

"Now, my dear adventurer," she said in an almost perfect imitation of Cinderella's singsongy voice, "come forward."

"Actually, I don't think I'm technically an adventurer anymore," I said as I came closer. A pang went through me at the words. Disobeying the Committee had been the only way to get my parents back, I reminded myself, even if it meant getting fired. Besides, maybe the fact that I wasn't actually an adventurer would prevent the queen from doing whatever creepy thing she had planned for me.

"No matter," the queen said. "You are still an adventurer in your heart."

Or maybe not.

She climbed a couple of stone steps and sat on top of a throne, her dress spreading out around her like a silvery cupcake. I couldn't believe I was standing face-to-face with the fairy who could very well have taken my parents. I didn't know whether I should scream at her for ruining my life or flatter her to get as much information as possible. Neither approach felt right.

"How are you enjoying my kingdom? Is it not beautiful?" she asked. Unlike the rest of her golden body, her eyes were dark and dull.

"Straight out of a fairy tale," I said.

That seemed to make her glow even more brightly. "After my father died, I made this land into what I always knew it could be." The queen motioned to the film that was still playing silently on the walls.

"A movie?" I said.

"Perfect," she corrected. "When my father ruled here, the fairies wasted their lives trying to please visitors." Her smile dimmed. "He made me go with him when I was a girl and shake hands with everyone who walked through those gates. It was disgraceful. I was a princess, and yet he made me act like a commoner. Can you imagine?"

I certainly *could* imagine what it was like to be a commoner.

"Then, one day, I saw this tale," she went on, pointing to the movie screen again. "For the first time in my life, I realized what a real princess could be."

"Couldn't you be a real princess and still keep the theme park open?" I said.

"Closing the park *proved* that I was a real princess. More than that: a true queen. Fairies are meant to be magical, beautiful creatures. By getting rid of that foul park, I gave our beauty back to us."

"Sorry to break it to you," I said, "but this place is still a theme park. I mean, you have characters wandering around in costumes and everyone treating the elevators like they're rides. It might not be full of roller coasters, but it's still an amusement park."

"Nonsense!" she said. "I will never continue my father's foolish ways."

I shrugged. "You already have."

Bing! "*The next mermaid water show is starting in ten minutes*," the announcement chirped.

"See?" I said smugly.

The queen looked ready to explode. Oops. I hadn't meant to get her all riled up, but I couldn't just stand there and let her go on kidding herself.

Then she sucked in a long breath and said, "No matter. When my prince finally comes, everything will be perfect." She closed her eyes and hummed a few notes from none other than "Someday My Prince Will Come."

I nearly choked. The queen really *was* crazy. "You know

that song is from *Snow White and the Seven Dwarfs*, don't you?" If you were going to have an unhealthy obsession with a movie, you should at least get the details right.

The queen acted like she hadn't heard me, though she finally stopped humming. Instead, she gazed at a glass display case in the middle of the room that I hadn't noticed before. Inside was a purple, velvet pillow. And on that pillow was a glass shoe. Instead of the usual glass slipper, this was a glass loafer that had clearly been made for a man.

"Um, is that for your prince?" I said.

The queen nodded. "I have searched through the entire kingdom for the one who fits that shoe, but I have not found him. One day, he will come, and I will finally have a prince to rule at my side."

I wasn't sure a future prince would want to put on a shoe that a thousand other guys had tried on. Besides, hadn't the queen ever heard of online dating?

"Or," she went on, "if I do not find my prince, then I will conjure him myself. Once I have him by my side, everything will truly be perfect." The queen's eyes swung toward me, and I saw the same hungry look on her face that I'd seen on Mahlia's. "And you will help me make that dream come true, Jenny the Adventurer."

"What are you talking about?" There was no way I was helping this glowing nutcase.

The queen stood and took a few steps toward me. I could practically feel the light drifting off her glowing skin. It sparkled like magic. Was that why she was all lit up? Was her body literally oozing with power?

"I have a proposal for you," she said. "It is simple, really. You give me what I want, and I give you what you want."

My heart clenched. Did she mean...? Were my parents...? I could barely even think the words. "What do you want?" I whispered.

"Oh, nothing much. Only how to find the Committee."

I laughed. She had to be kidding. "Have you *met* the Committee? Those old women are insane. Why would you want to be anywhere near them?"

The last trace of the queen's singsongy voice disappeared. "You have seen them," she hissed. "You know where they are. And you will tell me."

"I don't know anything. Their location is kept a secret. I can't even get there on my own. And even if I did know, why would I tell you?"

The queen smiled. "Because once you lead me to the Committee, I will return your parents to you."

Chapter Nine

They were here! They were really here! My parents were in Fairy Land!

I wanted to cartwheel around the room, but I had to keep calm. The queen obviously wanted to negotiate. I couldn't look too eager or she'd think she'd already won.

"Where are they?" I said. "Why have you been keeping them here all these years?"

The Queen Fairy didn't answer my question. Instead, she studied me for a long moment. "Will you bring me to the Committee's location or not?" she finally said.

"I already told you, I don't know where it is!"

"You know how to get there."

She was right. I did know how. Anthony could take me. Or Dr. Bradley—if he wasn't with the Committee already. Why wasn't she asking Anthony to bring her there? Why was she asking me? Then I realized: Anthony didn't have a gaping hole in his life like I did. The Queen Fairy knew I was willing to do anything to get my family back together.

"How do I know you're telling the truth?" I said, my excitement dimming. Maybe this was just a trick. "For all I know, you have no clue where my parents are."

The queen flashed another smile. Then she waved her hand, and the walls displaying *Cinderella* flickered and went dark. After a second, they began showing something completely different. A dimly lit room, two narrow beds, and on those beds, two sleeping people. A man and a woman.

All I could do was stare. They were older than I remembered, but it was them. My mom and dad.

"Where is that?" I whispered as sudden tears rolled down my cheeks. "Where are you keeping them?"

The fairy shook her head. "Remember, in order to get what you want, first you must give me what I want." She waved her hand again, and the screens went dark. My parents vanished.

I wiped my face with my fingers, trying to keep down the sobs that were threatening to burst out of me. My parents were alive. They were here. I'd finally found them. But to get them back, I would have to...

"Why do you want to see the Committee so badly?" I said. "I'm not agreeing to anything until you tell me."

She turned and went to sit back on her throne. Then she studied me, her dark eyes like two black holes in her glowing face. "I want to take their power, and I want them gone."

I stood totally frozen. This was crazy. I couldn't lead the Queen Fairy to the Committee members, not if she was going to suck up their magic like she'd done with the Land of Tales. I wasn't the Committee's biggest fan, but without those cranky old women around, things could get pretty chaotic. They were the ones responsible for keeping the magical worlds safe and organized.

But my parents…if I did this one thing, I would have my parents back. Then it would all be over and we could go home and have our lives back, just like I'd been dreaming about for seven years. Whatever the Queen Fairy was doing with my parents, she wasn't going to let them go without a fight, not after all this time. Maybe agreeing to this was the only way.

"What is your answer?" said the Queen Fairy.

I knew I should say no, that I should laugh in her face at the idea of betraying the Committee. But I couldn't say a word.

"Perhaps you need a few moments to consider my offer."

The queen snapped her fingers, and two golden cages appeared out of thin air. One cage was filled with dozens of mice of various sizes and colors. The other housed tons of small birds. All of them were dressed in tiny clothes.

What was going on?

"It is time to sing!" the queen announced to the animals.

I was probably imagining things, but it sounded like the mice and birds let out a collective sigh, as if singing was the last thing they wanted to do.

The Queen Fairy started belting out "Someday My Prince Will Come" again, and this time the birds twittered along while the mice chimed in with voices that reminded me of miniature kazoos.

Did the queen think this was going to help me make up my mind about her proposal? If anything, it was just making me even more confused (and giving me a headache). When she started dancing around the room with an imaginary partner, things had gone far enough.

"Stop it!" I yelled. "This isn't helping!"

The queen let out an impatient sigh and waved her hand. The woodland creatures and their cages instantly disappeared. "Very well. I will give you more time to decide."

"What if I won't do it?" I said, my voice cracking.

"Then I will keep you in my kingdom, just as I have kept your parents. None of you will ever see your home again. And I will find some other way to get to the Committee, so your refusal to help me will have been for nothing."

I thought of Trish, Melissa, and Aunt Evie. What would they do if I never came back? No. It wouldn't come to that. I'd find a way. I'd get my family and myself home.

But at what price? a small voice in my head asked.

"Go now," said the Queen Fairy. "You have three days to decide."

She turned away from me, and I drifted back toward the elevator like my legs were being controlled by someone else.

I had three days.

Chapter Ten

As I waited for the elevator, two of the queen's fairy body-guards beside me, I couldn't get the image of my sleeping parents out of my head. They were really here somewhere. Maybe in this very palace. I could be standing right above their heads. The thought made me want to scream and jump up and down at the same time.

The elevator finally arrived. I expected the leprechaun guards to be inside waiting to take me back to my room, but when the doors slid open, I found myself face-to-face with Ilda the witch. She was still dressed in the hideous sparkly, purple sweater she'd been wearing the last time I saw her, but her gray curls were matted and her orange lipstick was gone, leaving her lips pale and dry.

"Jenny," she said in a hoarse whisper. "I knew you'd follow me here."

"Silence," one of the leprechaun guards said, pushing

her out into the hallway. I realized Ilda's hands were bound in front of her. All that stuff Mahlia had said about Ilda being an honored guest had been a lie. The witch was a prisoner, just like me.

"Where are you taking her?" I said.

Karfum turned to the other guards. "I will stay here with the adventurer. Gold ahead and bring the prisoner to the queen."

The other leprechauns bowed their heads and pulled Ilda away while the fairy guards followed behind. I felt like I should say something to her, but what? Then the group disappeared around the corner, and she was gone.

"Is she going to be okay?" I asked Karfum. Ilda wasn't my favorite person in the universe—her mind games drove me insane—but if it weren't for the information she'd given me, I would have never figured out where my parents had gone.

Karfum sighed and twirled the shamrock between his lips. "The queen has lost patience with the witch. I suspect things will not gold well for her this time."

"What do you mean?"

A loud *Pop!* echoed from down the corridor. It was followed by loud, rodentlike squeaking. Uh-oh. I was afraid I knew what had just happened.

Needing to see the truth for myself, I turned and darted down the hall away from Karfum.

"Come back!" he yelled, but I didn't stop, not even when I heard the Queen's Guard running after me.

When I rounded the corner and emerged in the queen's throne room, I saw exactly what I'd been afraid of. In the Queen Fairy's hand was a small, gray-eared mouse in a tiny, purple sweater.

"What did you do to her?" I demanded just as Karfum caught up to me and grabbed my arm. The fairy guards quickly surrounded us.

"Quiet," Karfum whispered in my ear. "You'll only make things worse."

The queen didn't even look my way, like I was invisible. Instead, she conjured a golden cage and shoved Ilda inside. The gray-eared mouse tried to make a run for it, but its struggle was pointless. The cage slammed shut and disappeared.

I stood there staring at the empty spot where the cage had been. Then, feeling numb from head to toe, I let Karfum and another guard lead me away.

Ilda had been turned into a singing rodent, and it was my fault. If I hadn't convinced her to tell me about my parents' whereabouts, the queen would have never brought her here and punished her for revealing the truth to me.

Part of me knew it was crazy to feel sorry for Ilda when she'd helped the Queen Fairy steal all the magic from the Land of Tales. And yet, I couldn't help feeling guilty.

I was an adventurer. I was supposed to protect magical creatures, not stand by and watch them be transformed into rodents.

Then again, wasn't that what I was considering doing if I turned the Committee over to the Queen Fairy? If she had the Committee members under her thumb, she could turn every last magical creature into part of her musical act.

And it would be my fault.

I couldn't let that happen. But if I didn't do what the Queen Fairy said, then my only chance to get my parents back could be gone.

Chapter Eleven

After the guards led me back to my room, I sat on the bed staring out the window at the haze. My parents were somewhere in this city. I could almost *feel* them nearby.

Frustrated, I grabbed a mini-golf ball and chucked it against the wall. It bounced off the bathroom door and sailed into the toilet. *Plop!*

Oops.

As I sunk back on the bed, it occurred to me that if I could find where the fairies were hiding my mom and dad, maybe I could rescue them before the queen's deadline and be long gone by the time the three days were up.

In order to find my parents, I first had to get out of my room. I was tempted to try sneaking out through the panels in the closets, but my cuff would go off again. And this time, since the leprechauns wouldn't have to hurry to get me ready for an audience with the queen, I doubted they'd be so forgiving. Plus, I didn't exactly want to get zapped again.

Maybe there was another way. Whatever Luken had done to be able to sneak around the palace undetected, I needed to do it too. I crawled into the closet and tried tapping on the back of it a few times to see if he would answer, but there was no sound in the room next door. I'd just have to wait for him to come back.

As it got darker and darker outside, there was still no sign of Luken.

Chances were, he'd prowl through my room while I was sleeping, on his way to the tunnels. If I set a trap for him, maybe I could get him to help me.

I arranged things around the room until I was sure my trap was ready. Then, with nothing left to do, I got ready for bed.

After what felt like an hour of staring at the ceiling and wondering where my parents were, and what had happened to Dr. Bradley, and if Anthony was okay, I finally managed to fall asleep.

I wasn't usually a big dreamer, and when I did have dreams, they were full of things like half-troll, half-Pegasus hybrids and other wacky magical creatures that didn't exist.

This time, though, my dream felt like someone was showing me a movie of one of my adventures.

I was in the Land of Speak, the last mission I'd gone on before I found out that my parents had been adventurers (instead of dentists like I'd always thought). I was in the palace, talking to Prince Lamb—a mouthless magical sheep, turned cute human boy—about how to best defeat Klarr, the evil clown sorcerer. There was a sudden *Pop!* and my best friends, Trish and Melissa, appeared in the middle of the throne room, insisting that Klarr was about to come and attack us. I tried to tell them that they shouldn't be here, that they were supposed to be in the Land of Tales helping the villagers learn to live without magic, but they wouldn't listen to me.

As Klarr's clown car approached the palace, we rushed around gathering everyone we could find to help us fight. All of a sudden, I had the eerie feeling that someone was watching me. When I glanced over my shoulder, there was no one there.

The longer the dream went on, the more it felt like whoever was watching me was actually inside my brain, somehow looking into my thoughts. I had a prickling sensation at the back of my skull that just kept getting worse and worse.

Finally, it got so bad that I couldn't stand it anymore. "I want to wake up now," my dream-self said.

And I did. Just like that. As if I'd pulled myself out of the dream by snapping my fingers. That had definitely never happened to me before.

I sat up on the uncomfortably stiff fairy bed, in my uncomfortably starchy fairy pajamas, and a huge wave of homesickness washed over me. I'd been away from home dozens of times on my adventures, and it had never bothered me before. Anthony had always made sure my aunt didn't notice I was gone so she wouldn't worry.

This time, all I wanted was to be in my own room in my own bed. I wanted to be able to pick up the phone and call Trish and Melissa and hear their voices. Or to chat with Aunt Evie over a nice cup of Earl Grey tea while one of her animal patients snoozed on the table. Heck, I would have settled for talking to Anthony about his latest candy obsession, but even that was out of the question since I was trapped in my room. The only sign of life outside my prison was the faint sound of mice singing somewhere below, which didn't make me feel any better.

The truth was, I wanted my parents back in my life so badly that it hurt. I had to figure out how to make that happen. I just had to.

Chapter Twelve

Just as the sun was starting to come up, a huge *Crash!* echoed through my room.

The trap I'd set had caught a Luken-sized intruder.

"Ow!" he cried as he tried to untangle himself from the web of bath towels and mini-golf clubs I'd crisscrossed in front of the closet.

"Sneaking around again?" I said, turning on the lights.

Luken struggled to get free, causing a shower of mini-golf balls to fall on his head. "Some help, please?"

"Fine," I said, "but you have to tell me how you manage to sneak around this place. How do you keep that cuff from going off?"

"Sorry. I cannot reveal that information."

I crossed my arms in front of my chest. "Then you can get out of that mess on your own."

One last ball bounced off Luken's forehead. He sighed. "Very well, but you must tell no one my secret."

"I won't." As I helped free him from the trap I'd made, he told me how he'd deactivated his tracking cuff by opening it up and switching off some kind of sensor. Yet another bit of technology that made no sense in a fairy-tale land.

"Switching the cuffs off is rather simple, really," Luken said.

"Okay, so can you deactivate mine?" I said, unwinding the last towel from around his arm.

Luken shook his head. "It is too dangerous. If anyone finds out what I have done, I will be harshly punished. I cannot inflict that same fate on you."

"You don't understand. I don't care how much they punish me! If I don't get out of my room and find my parents in the next two days, then I might never get them back. Please, you have to help me!" I was about a second away from grabbing him and shaking him until his pointy ears fell off.

"What do you mean?" Luken asked. "What has happened to your parents?"

"They've been missing since I was really young, and now I know the queen has them hidden somewhere. She said she'd make a deal with me, but I don't trust her. That's why I want to find my parents on my own, so I can get them out of here before the queen's deadline is up."

He stared at me. "You have actually *met* the Queen Fairy? What was she like?"

"Creepy and blinding. I can still kind of see her outline on the back of my eyelids every time I blink."

Luken's face lit up, and he pulled out his sketch pad again. This time, his drawing was of a ride made completely out of lights. No doubt it would blind everyone who went through it, probably permanently.

When he saw me looking at the sketch, Luken quickly closed his notebook and put it away.

"The queen has ruined many families," he said, rubbing one of his long ears. "If helping you means that at least one family might be reunited, then I suppose it is worth the risk."

"You mean you'll do it?" I practically squealed. "Thank you!"

Luken shrugged. "I only hope it will help."

He looked so sad all of a sudden that my excitement faded. "Did she break up your family too?" I said.

He nodded slowly, not looking at me. "Before I was

born, my father was one of the most influential theme-park designers in this land. His sketches inspired the Ferris wheel and many other rides, and he was working on his biggest project yet: a ship that could actually take you into space. Can you imagine something so incredible?"

Actually, I could. But Luken was so awed by the idea that I didn't say so. Instead, I asked: "So what happened?"

"The Carousel Catastrophe," Luken whispered like it hurt to even say the words. "My father and several others perished in the accident. The queen had just come into power, and she used the tragedy as an excuse to close the park once and for all."

"I'm so sorry," I said. "And your mom?"

"After the accident, she came to believe that our theme-park lifestyle was responsible for my father's death and that something would happen to me too if I followed in his footsteps. She became one of the queen's biggest support-ers, convinced that her vision for the future of this land was the only way to keep me safe."

"You don't agree with her?'

Luken shook his head. "My father's designs were amaz-ing. If we can get the park to reopen, then I will be able to carry on his legacy and make others happy just like he did."

"That's why you're always drawing plans for amusement park rides?" I said.

He smiled shyly. "They are not nearly as good as my father's were, but most of his plans were destroyed. I hope to one day be able to replace them all." His smile faded. "That is why the queen must be taken off her throne, so that we can reopen the park and return this land to the way it should be."

"Okay, then we'll make that happen. If you help me find my parents, I'll help you take down that glowing fairy." I stuck out my hand. "Deal?"

Luken stared at my hand for a minute and then lightly rubbed his palm against mine. I guess that was the closest to a fairy handshake I was going to get. "Deal," he said.

I held out my cuff. "Now, please turn this thing off."

Luken reached into his pocket and took out a small box filled with tools. He got to work, poking and prodding at the cuff. "If we are to search for your parents," he said, "we should do it soon. There is a lot of unrest in the kingdom."

"What do you mean?"

After glancing around, as if making sure no one was listening, Luken whispered: "Protests. The leprechauns are going on strike early tomorrow morning. They will refuse to go to their stations."

"That's perfect!" I said. "It'll be a huge distraction. The fairies will be so worried about what's going on with the leprechauns that no one will notice if we're not in our rooms."

Luken nodded, rubbing his ear again. I was starting to think he did that whenever he was pondering something. "That might work."

There was a loud knock on the door.

Luken grabbed his tools and jumped to his feet. "At dawn," he whispered, hurrying toward the closet he'd just come from. "When the leprechauns strike, we shall go into the tunnels." Then he disappeared.

Chapter Thirteen

When the door opened, Karfum and the two female leprechauns who'd given me a makeover bustled into my room.

"What's going on?" I said.

"It's time to get you ready for the ball."

Oh no. I'd totally forgotten about the ball Mahlia had mentioned. Maybe my brain had blocked it out on purpose. The last thing I wanted to do was watch fairies waltzing around.

"Do I have to go?" I said.

The leprechauns didn't answer. Instead, they bustled me across the room and started attacking my hair again. I didn't know how celebrities put up with teams of stylists fussing over them all the time. Then again, my friend Melissa would have been in heaven.

As the two female leprechauns worked on recurling my hair, Karfum smeared green paste all over my face that smelled like it was made out of crushed-up clover.

"What is that?" I said.

"A shamrock mask," he said. "It helps hydrate the skin." Then he dipped his finger into the leftover paste and licked it. "Plus, it tastes delightful."

Gross.

When I was all made up and dressed in a gown that made me feel like a pink cream puff, the guards ushered me out into the hallway where Anthony and a few other leprechauns were already waiting.

I almost fell over when I saw Anthony's outfit. He was dressed in a green vest and green tights, and his shirt and pants were the exact same color as his orange hair. He could have passed for a walking pumpkin. Somehow, the leprechauns had managed to slick back Anthony's unruly hair, and they'd even woven a green ribbon into his orange beard. I could tell the gnome was not happy about his makeover by the way he was angrily crunching on a hunk of purple candy.

I wanted to pull Anthony aside and tell him about the queen's proposal, but I didn't get a chance. The guards ushered us to the elevator, and then we all screamed our way up to one of the top floors. This time, I threw up my arms and shrieked as loudly as I could. It felt good to get some of my frustrations out. Maybe that's why the leprechauns didn't mind sticking to this particular rule. If someone took my gold and trapped me in another land, I'd be screaming as much as possible too.

We went down a hallway where an overly chipper leprechaun told us to stand in front of a forest backdrop and smile for a contraption that could have been a toaster oven.

"Perfect!" the leprechaun called as he handed over a photo of me scowling and Anthony grinning like a fool. "Would you like to take one as a souvenir?"

"Um, no thanks," I said, just as Anthony snatched the picture out of my hand and happily put it in his pocket.

Mahlia and the Queen Fairy had both insisted this land was no longer a theme park, but either they were blind or totally fooling themselves. Only amusement parks and cruise ships forced you to take touristy photos, and last I checked, the floor wasn't swaying under our feet.

When we got to the ballroom, it was decked out in silvery lights and white garlands. The room was filled with fairies, all dressed in ball gowns and fancy suits (all with tights, of course) and all dancing stiffly to deafening music that sounded like cats marching across cellos.

"Wow!" said Anthony. "Look at this shindig. Promise you'll save me a dance, Jenny-girl."

"Trust me. That's a really bad idea. I'm a horrible dancer." Even my gym teacher had asked me to sit out our last square-dancing unit so no one would get hurt.

As the guards ushered Anthony and me across the room, I kept an eye out for the Queen Fairy. She had to be here somewhere. This was her ball, after all. But there was no sign of her. Maybe she was watching from one of the shadowy balconies around the room.

The crowd parted to let us by, but I could feel the fairies' eyes on us. I started to notice that even though the fairies were all dressed up, there was something off about each of them. One woman's hair was only half done. Another's dress was different colors in a way that made me wonder if she'd run out of fabric dye. One man's coattails were two lengths, as if one of them had stopped growing before the other, and he was only wearing part of a top hat.

I turned to Karfum. "Why does everyone look so... unfinished?"

"Not enough magic," he said. "The rations only let them do so much."

Again, I thought of the queen and the magic nearly

bursting out of her. How could the other fairies stand having theirs rationed when she had so much? Or maybe they didn't know about all her magic. Maybe that's why the Queen Fairy stayed hidden away.

Anthony let out a giggle beside me. "Look, Jenny-girl," he said, pointing to the display case in the middle of the room with the glass loafer inside it. Apparently, the queen liked to bring the case with her wherever she went. "That shoe looks like it's my size."

I had to laugh too. "If it is, that means you're the Queen Fairy's true prince," I said.

Anthony's eyes widened. "Really?"

"Listen," I said. "Speaking of the queen, I need to tell you something—"

Trumpets blared from somewhere high over our heads. Then Mahlia appeared in the doorway, and everyone stopped dancing and bowed. Only when she took a few steps forward did I notice there was someone next to her.

Luken.

He was dressed up even fancier than usual and looked pretty cute for an alien fairy. He stood at Mahlia's side with a fake grin on his face, her hand resting on his arm as if he were her date. Or…

"Her son," I said softly.

"What?" said Anthony, drooling in the direction of a table of fairy food in the corner.

"Nothing," I said, but my mind was spinning. All that stuff Luken had told me about his parents, about his mom supporting the queen after his dad died, it had all been about Mahlia.

When he glanced across the room, Luken's eyes met mine, and his fake smile faded. Clearly, he hadn't expected to see me here. Then he turned away, as if we were complete strangers, and started talking to another fairy.

I told myself the disappointment I felt was stupid. Of course Luken couldn't let on that he knew me. Besides, we'd only just met. So what if he was ignoring me? So what if he hadn't told me who his mother was? Okay, so maybe I'd thought we'd had a real connection when he'd confessed that his family had also been torn apart by the Queen Fairy. I'd thought I could really trust him. Now I wasn't so sure.

"Everyone dance!" a voice echoed from high above us. I recognized it as the queen's. She was still hidden away, but she was watching.

Everyone scrambled to find a dance partner. I realized this was my chance to finally talk to Anthony.

"Hey!" he said as I pulled him out onto the dance floor. "I thought you didn't dance."

"I'm making an exception," I said, trying not to step on his feet. "I have to tell you something. The queen offered me a deal."

Anthony gave me a quick spin and then had to catch me before I collided with an old fairy couple. "What kind of deal?" he said.

I quietly told him about my conversation with the queen. "She gave me three days to decide," I said when I'd recapped her offer, "and now I only have two days left."

"Ow!" Anthony cried as I accidentally kicked him in the elbow. "So what are you going to do?"

"I don't know!" I said, managing to step on my own feet this time. "Of course I want my parents back, but what about the magical worlds?"

Anthony shrugged and then shimmied his shoulders. "I can't make that decision for you, Jenny-girl. You have to do what you think is right."

If only I knew what that was. Having my own happy ending was starting to seem impossible.

As the song ended, Anthony wrenched out of my grip and ran toward the snack table before I could force him into another dance. Just then, Mahlia came up to me and gave me her trademark fake smile.

"You dance beautifully," she said.

"Um, thanks," I said, wondering if she needed glasses. My feet hurt from how many times I'd managed to step on them. I couldn't imagine how Anthony's legs, arms, and shoulders felt.

Mahlia's smile faded. "The queen has told me about her offer," she said. Her voice dropped to a whisper. "Take it. It is your only chance." Then she strode away, leaving me alone in the crowd.

"Jenny-girl!" Anthony cried after a minute. I glanced over to find him next to the display case, grinning like a maniac. Somehow, he'd managed to wrench the case open. He was holding up his foot, which he'd shoved into the glass loafer. "Look. It fits perfectly!"

The music screeched to a stop and all eyes swung to look at Anthony.

From above, the queen's voice rang out again: "Bring him to me."

Fairy guards appeared out of nowhere and grabbed Anthony's arms. Before I could do anything—*Pop!*—they vanished, leaving only one of Anthony's worn shoes behind.

Chapter Fourteen

"Where did they take him?" I demanded, marching over to Karfum. Around me, the ball started up again as if Anthony hadn't just disappeared.

"Nothing to be worried about."

"Of course I'm worried!" I said. "He's my friend, and the queen just abducted him because she thinks he's her prince. You know he can't really be her prince, right? I mean, you've met him!"

Karfum's mouth twitched, like he was trying not to smile.

"Please, can you just make sure he's okay?" I could easily imagine the queen getting tired of Anthony and turning him into a tap-dancing penguin or something.

The leprechaun let out a soft sigh and nodded. "I will see what I can find out."

"Thank you. Now, can you please get me out of here? I can't stand being at this ball a second longer."

"Attendance is mandatory for all fairies and their honored guests," said Karfum.

"Okay, so I attended. Now I'd like to go."

He glanced around, as if making sure no one was listening. Then he whispered, "Act ill."

It was exactly the kind of idea I'd normally come up with. In fact, I was surprised I hadn't thought of it myself. I guess being in Fairy Land, knowing that my parents were so close by, had started to get to me. I'd barely even said anything cheesy since I'd been here!

I grabbed my stomach and started groaning.

"What are you doing?" said Karfum.

"Acting sick."

He shook his head and pointed to the dance floor. "It looks like you're doing the latest dance."

I glanced over my shoulder to see lots of fairies crouched down, holding their stomachs and groaning in time to the music.

"Okay, then what do you suggest?" I asked.

Karfum glanced around. Then he gently nudged the back of my knee so that I fell forward. "Hey!" I cried, just as he caught me before I hit the floor.

"Looks like you're feeling faint," he said loudly. "Better

get you back to your quarters." He made a big show of walking me to the elevator, politely declining offers of help from the other guards. "I'll take care of her. Just too much dancing in one night."

When we were in the elevator, Karfum finally let go of me, and I gave him a grateful smile. I expected him to launch into the usual screaming as the elevator started to go down. Instead, he leaned in and whispered: "Don't let the queen control you. I've allowed her to trap me, but you have a choice."

"So do you," I said. "What if we got your pot of gold back? Then you could leave too."

He shook his head. "I'm not worried about myself. I only care about my children."

I remembered him mentioning a son and a daughter, but I hadn't seen either of them. "Are they here in Fairy Land?"

He sighed. "I can't be sure. I have four children, three girls and a boy. One by one, they've gone missing since we were brought here. And now my boy, Belthum…" Karfum wiped his eyes. "He's gone too."

"Belthum's your son?" I said, remembering the leprechaun friend Luken had mentioned.

Karfum's eyes snapped up. "You know him? You've seen him?"

"No," I said. "But Luken is trying to find him."

Karfum sighed again. "Those two have been friends for years. I didn't like my son being around that fairy boy, no matter how different he is from his mother. I thought their friendship would at least keep Belthum safe, but I guess I was wrong."

"Do you think he's been moused?"

"I hope so." Karfum rubbed his temples. "Because at least that means there's still hope."

Seeing the leprechaun look so defeated made anger flare up inside me. He had so much more power than I did in this place. How could he just give up? "You're going to let the queen take your whole family and not do anything about it?" I said.

"What else can I do?" he said. "Before we were brought here, I was a simple shamrock farmer. I knew nothing of being a guard! Then the queen brought us here and took our pots of gold...and then my children began to disappear..." He shook his head. "I thought being the head guard would give me more access to the kingdom, help me find them. Instead, it has just made me even more under the queen's thumb. I am powerless!"

He put his head in his hands and started to weep. I had no idea what to do, so finally I channeled Aunt Evie and patted his head as if he were a kitten.

"It'll be okay," I said. "Even miracles take a little time." I clapped my hand over my mouth. I was pretty sure I'd just quoted a line from the cartoon version of *Cinderella*! This place was seriously starting to wheedle its way into my brain.

Karfum let out a shuddering sigh and wiped his tears away with one of his shamrock handkerchiefs. "You're right," he said. "I must be strong. Before he disappeared, Belthum was working with Pryll and others to organize against the queen. I don't agree with their methods, but perhaps if I help them…"

I thought back to the warning Pryll had asked Karfum to deliver to the queen. At least someone in this kingdom was trying to stand up to her. "Don't worry," I said. "We'll find out what happened to your son, and we'll get rid of the queen. I mean, Cinderella isn't supposed to be the bad guy, right?"

Karfum just shrugged at me, but I didn't need an answer. The Queen Fairy had taken my parents; she'd taken Karfum's whole family away from him; and now she'd even taken Anthony. There was no way I was going to let her get away with it.

As we got out of the elevator, I realized we were on the lowest level of the palace. The hallway was dark and musty, and the air was eerily still.

"Where are we?" I said.

"Oh," said Karfum. "My mistake. I should not have brought you here." Instead of closing the elevator door, though, he just stood by quietly. There was obviously something here he wanted me to see.

I poked my head out into the hallway and squinted through the shadows. One end of the hallway was a dead end, but I spotted a door in the other direction. In front of it were half a dozen heavily armed fairy guards.

"What's down there?" I whispered. What kind of place would need to be guarded as carefully as the queen herself?

"Nothing," said Karfum, sucking on the end of his ever-present shamrock. "We have stayed here too long." He herded me back into the elevator like the building was on fire.

As we screamed on the way up the elevator, my brain was buzzing. The fairies were definitely hiding something.

Chapter Fifteen

The rest of the evening passed in a blur of nothingness, and finally it was night. I tried to stay awake so I'd be ready when Luken came, and also to keep from having any other weird dreams. No such luck.

My eyelids got impossibly heavy, and I slipped into another dream that felt like real life.

This time, I was in the middle of the very first adventure I'd ever been sent on. I was in a charred forest, trying to convince the dragon king to stop fighting with the pixies over pieces of furniture. Suddenly, Aunt Evie appeared and accused me of hiding my adventurer identity from her. I begged her to forgive me, but she was so hurt that I'd lied to her that she refused to listen to my apologies. Then I got that feeling again, the prickling at the back of my skull that made me think someone was rummaging around in my brain.

Before I could wake myself up, I heard somebody calling my name and a quiet knocking nearby.

My eyes flew open. It took me a minute to totally wake up and realize I was in my fairy room, sprawled on the bed, wearing the ridiculous cream-puff dress. Since the guards had taken my regular clothes, it was the only outfit I had.

I let Luken out of the closet, still feeling shaken by the dream. It had seemed so real, like I'd actually been in the forest talking to my aunt. But that didn't matter now.

"Is the leprechaun strike starting already?" I said, fighting back a yawn. It seemed way too dark outside to be anywhere near morning.

Luken shook his head. "Not until dawn, but this could not wait."

"What is it? What's wrong?" I was wide awake now.

"There is a meeting in the Magical Village that we must attend. Someone there might have information about your parents' location."

I remembered the cluster of narrow streets we'd passed by on our way into the city, where Pryll had delivered his warning. "What kind of meeting?"

Luken just shook his head and claimed it wasn't safe to give me any more information.

"When the leprechauns go on strike, we need to search the lower level," I said, thinking of the guarded door I'd seen earlier. "I'm pretty sure the queen is hiding something there."

He nodded and waved me into the closet. As we crawled through the hidden panel, I held my breath, half expecting my cuff to go off like it had before. Luckily, whatever Luken had done to disable the tracking device worked, and we got to the hallway near the elevators without a problem.

Luken felt around in the corner for a minute before a panel popped open. "The tunnel entrances often run alongside elevator shafts," he whispered.

I peered down into the panel and chuckled. I'd been imagining the tunnels as actual, you know, *tunnels*. In fact, they were more like slides.

"Wait, I know what this is," I whispered as we climbed in. "We're in an old water ride."

"A water ride?" said Luken.

"Yeah, it's a—ahhhhhh!" Some kind of magic grabbed me and made me whoosh down the slide, twisting me this way and that, until I thought my stomach might turn inside out. I heard Luken sliding down behind me. My poufy dress tried to blow up over my head the entire way. Fairy fashion was *not* designed for adventurers.

Not that I was an adventurer anymore, I reminded myself. The Committee had probably filed all the official paperwork to have me fired by now. That meant I was just a regular girl again…a regular girl who was trying to rescue her parents from a delusional, glowing fairy.

Finally, we rounded a sharp corner and crash-landed onto a mattress that was tucked behind what looked like an oversized air-conditioner.

I staggered to my feet and smoothed down my gown, feeling like I'd just been sucked through a tornado. "How come you have to take the tunnels at all?" I asked. "Can't you just use your magic to transport yourself around the kingdom?"

"No," he said flatly. "I cannot."

I wondered if I'd stumbled on yet another touchy subject. Apparently, everyone in Fairy Land had tons of them.

Luken quietly shut a panel in the wall. "The panels that lead to the tunnels are the same throughout the palace," he whispered. "They blend in easily with their surroundings, but once you know their size and shape, they are simple to find."

"Thanks," I said, hoping I'd never have to locate one of the panels on my own. Luken could claim they were easy to find, but I could barely see the door even though I knew exactly where it was. "Where are we?" The air in the tunnel was so damp that it smelled like seaweed.

"Deep under the palace," said Luken, "in a system of passageways left over from the days when this land was a theme park. They have all since been sealed off, but the fairies once used them to go between attractions without being seen by the public."

"Oh, like at Disney World," I said. "I heard that's how they keep people from seeing Mickey wandering around without his head on." I smiled, thinking of how terrified Anthony had been of the troll in the headless troll costume.

Luken stopped and, not surprisingly, pulled out his sketchbook. I was willing to bet whatever ride he was drawing, it had to do with headless creatures.

Sure enough, when he shyly showed me the drawing after he was done, it looked a lot like the "It's a Small World" ride at Disney. Except that in Luken's version, all the little kids were headless. It was totally creepy.

"This is, um, interesting and all, but didn't you say we have a meeting to get to?" I asked.

"Right." He put away his sketch pad and waved me down a corridor that felt especially damp. I held up my dress to keep from getting slimy water all over the hem. Why, look at that. I was turning into a real lady.

"So," I said, finally asking the question that had been hanging in the air between us ever since he'd appeared in my room, "why didn't you tell me Mahlia was your mother?"

He sighed. "I knew you would not trust me if I told you her identity."

"It's not that. But it does kind of change things, you know? I mean, how can I be sure you won't take her side?"

"Because she is wrong!" he cried. "My mother has turned her back on everything my father believed in. He used our ability to see into people's dreams to help make Fairy Land the most amazing theme park in the magical worlds. And now all that is gone."

"Wait. Fairies can see into people's dreams?" Honestly, the idea didn't really surprise me. After all, the dreams I'd been having the past couple of days had clued me in that something strange was going on.

Luken sighed. "I should not have told you that." Then he hurried his steps so that I had to run to keep up with his long legs.

Chapter Sixteen

We wove our way through the tunnels, passing pieces of old rides and sections of faded theater sets until finally we came to a ladder that ran along the mossy wall. Luken went first and then helped pull me through a manhole. We emerged into the night air behind a bakery that could have been right out of a storybook. This had to be the Magical Village.

We tiptoed down one shadowy alley after another, until Luken stopped behind a small cobbler's shop and knocked on the door. Instantly, the door flew open, and Pryll glared back at us with his one eye.

"What is *she* doing here?" he said, pointing at me.

"Jenny is here to help," said Luken. Then he sauntered past Pryll as if the people eater were a stuffed animal instead of a menacing beast. I held my head high and followed Luken. Pryll grunted in annoyance but didn't try to stop me.

Inside the shop, I spotted pixies, trolls, mermaids, a few leprechauns, and even a couple of fairies crowded together. On the other side of the room, Karfum was standing next to another leprechaun guard. He caught my eye and gave me a small nod. I guess our conversation in the elevator had helped to change his mind about helping Pryll and the other rebels.

I expected Pryll to step forward and start the meeting. Instead, Luken was the one who stood in front of the crowd and said in a strong voice, "Thank you all for coming. Before we begin, I must report that Belthum has gone missing."

"Missing?" someone said with a gasp. "Does that mean this group has been compromised?"

"No," said Luken. "I am confident that Belthum did not give up any information about us. However, we must act quickly before our plans are discovered." He cleared his throat. "That is why the leprechauns will go on strike at dawn, and I would like you all to join in. This will be an opportunity for the creatures of this land to stand up to the queen together."

"It's too dangerous," one of the pixies squeaked. "The queen will punish us."

"Not if we team up," said a leprechaun. "We are her work force. She depends on us. If we all gold on strike at once, she will have to listen."

"Perhaps we can reason with her," one of the fairies said. Her thin shoulders were stooped, and her green skin was old and weathered. "She used to be a great leader."

Pryll snorted. "I don't care how many promises she made after the king died. Now all she thinks about is controlling everything we do. Forget striking. We need to attack!"

"That's foolish," said Karfum, stepping forward. Everyone turned to look at him, obviously surprised to hear him speak up. "Fighting won't get us anywhere. We don't have enough magic."

"No, *we* don't," said Pryll, with a snarl. "She took ours away, but you leprechauns still have magic. You just won't share it with us."

The crowd erupted in whispers. Obviously, the fact that only the leprechauns and fairies were allowed to keep some of their magic in this land was a big issue.

Luken raised his hand, and the creatures quieted. He was younger than everyone else in the room, but it was obvious they respected what he had to say. "Even if all the leprechauns and fairies on our side used their magic at once, it would not be enough to bring down the queen. Resisting peacefully is the only way."

Pryll grumbled to himself, but he didn't argue. I guess that meant Luken was right.

"We have come too far to turn back now," Luken continued. "The leprechaun strike will start at dawn as planned. If others care to join in, they are welcome."

The room erupted in heated whispers again. Beside me, Luken sighed. "I have tried for a long time to encourage everyone to band together against the queen," he said softly to me, "but they are unwilling to cooperate."

"Don't worry," I said. "I can handle this." After all, getting magical creatures to work together was kind of my specialty. Once I got the bickering under control, then I could finally ask if anyone knew where the queen was keeping my parents. "Hey, guys!"

Everyone turned to look at me.

"I know standing up to the queen is scary," I said. "Obviously, she's pretty powerful. But if you all work together, it'll pay off. I know it."

Pryll scrunched up his purple face. "How do you know? The leprechauns can strike all they want, but that doesn't mean it'll help the rest of us."

"It will pay off if you help each other out. Remember, there's no 'I' in team!" I waited for my cheesy saying to work its magic as usual, but everyone just kept staring at me.

"Um, no pain, no gain!" I tried again.

Still nothing.

"Er...you catch more flies with honey than with vinegar?" I said, desperate.

"What's honey?" one of the mermaids asked.

Wow. Tough crowd. Was I starting to lose my touch? Or had all those citywide announcements made the residents of Fairy Land immune to my cheesy sayings?

Before I could try anything else, pounding erupted at the door to the shop. *Bam! Bam! Bam!* "Queen's Guard. Open up!"

Everyone's faces turned panicked.

"We have been discovered!" cried Luken.

I started to run toward a nearby window, thinking we might be able to climb through it, but someone grabbed my arm before I could get there. *Pop!* The chaos around me faded, and I was sucked into a whirlpool of glittery green.

Chapter Seventeen

When I opened my eyes, I realized that I was back in my room in the palace. Karfum was holding on to my arm with one hand and Luken's wrist with the other.

"Thank you for bringing us to safety," said Luken. "If we had been caught..." He didn't need to finish that thought. No doubt we would have been swiftly turned into woodland creatures. Or worse, made to reenact scenes from *Cinderella*.

Karfum nodded briskly. "Try to get some rest."

"Wait," Luken said. "Will you join the strike in the morning?"

The leprechaun sighed. "Yes. Not because I think it will help, but because I know it is what Belthum would want me to do." Then he gave us a tight-lipped smile, twirled the shamrock between his lips, and slipped out into the hallway.

Luken turned to me. "I shall return at dawn, and we will explore the lower levels." Then he disappeared into the closet.

My heart was still beating at twice its usual rate. I didn't think I could fall asleep anytime soon. Instead, I sat on my bed, staring out the window at the shimmering haze that glowed even in the middle of the night.

Bing! I got ready for another one of the chipper announcements. Apparently, the fairies liked to make them at all hours. But the voice that chimed in over the intercom wasn't the one I'd been expecting.

"*Hey there, Fairy Land folks!*" Anthony's voice rang out from the speakers. "*Just a reminder that tomorrow is Official Candy Day, so make sure to bring candy with you to work!*"

Then the intercom fell silent. What was Anthony doing? At least he'd sounded okay, but was he actually on the queen's side now? I couldn't imagine there was enough candy in the universe to convince him to help her.

As I spread out on the bed, the queen's ultimatum kept bouncing around in my head. I had less than two days to decide whether or not to reveal the Committee's location. Less than two days to find my parents, get home, and put this entire glittering nightmare behind me.

* * *

Just as light was starting to come through the window, voices erupted in the hallway right outside my room.

I pressed my ear to the door and heard shouts, grunts, and marching footsteps fill the corridor.

"What are you doing?" I heard a fairy ask.

"Tell the queen we will not work until our demands are met," a leprechaun answered. "She must return our pots of gold, pay us real wages, and let us return to our land whenever we like. Until then we will not gold back to our posts."

The strike had officially begun.

A minute later, Luken appeared in my room. "Are you ready?" he asked.

I nodded and followed him toward the tunnels. Instead of using the same tunnel as the night before, we darted past the elevators to a tunnel entrance on the other side of the building. This time, as we climbed onto the slide, I made sure to wrap my full skirt around my legs so it would stay in place. We whooshed down until we were spit out onto a cold floor in the lower levels.

Luken took my hand with his thin fingers and pulled me toward a dark hallway as if he thought we didn't have time to waste. And he was right. Even if the fairies were distracted by the leprechaun strike, who knew how long it would be before they realized we weren't in our rooms. We had to find out what the fairies were hiding before they discovered we were gone.

Finally, we came to the same mysterious, guarded door I'd seen earlier. This time, there were no heavily armed fairies in front of it. They were probably off trying to force the leprechauns back to work. Not surprisingly, though, the door was locked.

"Now what?" I whispered.

Luken smiled and took out a homemade device that looked like a multipronged toothpick. He pushed it into the lock and gave it a few twists. A minute later, the door clicked open.

"One of my father's designs," he whispered, slipping the lock pick back into his pocket.

We crept into a dimly lit hallway with rows and rows of small, glass cells on either side. It was cold and deafeningly quiet. Something about the hushed atmosphere made me think of a hospital ward, but no hospital would ever be humming with this much magic. I could feel the hair on my head trying to stick up on end from the static pull of all that power.

"Where are we?" I whispered.

"I have heard my mother refer to a lab," said Luken. "She must have meant this place."

As we crept down the hallway, I realized that all of the cells were occupied. In each one, a prisoner lay on a small cot, perfectly still except for the steady rhythm of his or her breathing.

"Are they all asleep?" I said as we went from one pane of glass to the next.

"Their breathing is synchronized," Luken said. "It seems too unnatural to be regular sleep."

He was right. Everyone we passed was inhaling and exhaling at the exact same time. If we'd been in a cartoon, I would've expected them to be snoring in unison too. But this wasn't a cartoon. This was something much, much weirder.

Suddenly, the hallway filled with the sound of laughter.

Luken and I both whirled around, ready to run. Then I realized that the laughter had come from inside the cells. All the sleeping people had laughed at exactly the same time. What was going on here?

"Perhaps they are all having the same dream," said Luken as the laughter died down.

That was impossible, wasn't it? The prisoners weren't hooked up to any wires or tubes that I could see. Then again, if the fairies could see into people's dreams, maybe they could control them too. I shuddered, remembering how strange my dreams had been the past couple nights.

The hall filled with echoes again, but this time the sleeping figures weren't laughing. They were whimpering.

"We have to get everyone out of here," I said.

Luken shook his head. "There is nothing we can do, Jenny. This place is secured with the strongest kind of magic. We must keep exploring, before we are discovered. Perhaps we can find something that will help them."

I hated to admit that he was right. There was no way we could compete with the amount of magic that was coursing through this place. The cell doors were sealed with so much magic that they were actually glowing. If we so much as touched them, we'd become two deep-fried mozzarella sticks.

Leaving all these prisoners behind felt wrong, but we didn't have a choice.

We hurried down the hallway, passing more and more cells. They were mostly filled with fairies and leprechauns, but I spotted a few gnomes, sprites, and humans. What had these creatures done to get themselves locked up here? Could they be the adventurers who'd gone missing?

Then we came to a cell that was twice the size of the others. Inside, two cots were set up next to each other. On one cot, a small woman was spread out, her long hair pooled like a halo around her head. On the other was a thin man with a short beard covering his angular cheeks.

I stared at the two people. And stared and stared.

"Jenny," I vaguely heard Luken whisper, "we must keep moving."

I didn't move a muscle. I couldn't. My legs felt like they'd been stapled to the floor.

After all this time, after all these years, I had finally found my mom and dad.

Chapter Eighteen

"Jenny, what are you doing?" said Luken, tugging on my arm. "We must go."

"It's them," I whispered. "I found them." I started to put my hand on the glowing glass of the cell, my fingers shaking, but Luken grabbed my wrist and yanked it away.

"Are you mad?" he said. "That amount of magic could kill you!" Then the anger on Luken's face melted away as he glanced inside the cell. "These are your parents."

I nodded. My parents. They were really here. The image the queen had shown me was real.

"Mom!" I cried, finding my voice. "Dad!"

"Jenny, stop!" Luken hissed. "Someone will hear you. We must go."

I ignored him. I had to get to them. I had to make sure they were okay.

Frantic, I ripped off my sneaker and chucked it at the

cell door. It hit the glass with a *dzzzz* that sounded like a fly in a bug zapper. The shoe fell onto the floor, every part of it glowing. When the light faded, my formerly white sneaker was black and charred.

I grabbed the shoe again, ready to throw it as many times as it took to get some of the magic to wear off. If that didn't work, I'd start throwing my whole body against the cell door.

Luken grabbed my shoulders. "Jenny, please. The fairies will find us, and then you will be able to do nothing to help your parents."

I wanted to scream at him to leave me alone, that I wasn't going anywhere until my parents were free, but he was right. I couldn't break into the cell, and the last thing we needed was to get caught. Then I'd never have a chance to come back here.

As I took a step away from the glass, my head was spinning like I'd been holding my breath for too long. Even as I pulled my burned shoe back onto my foot, I couldn't stop looking at my parents. Before I knew it, tears were trickling down my face.

"Are you unwell?" said Luken, like he'd never seen tears before. It wouldn't surprise me if fairies never cried.

"No, I'm…I'm…" I didn't know what I was. "We have to get them out of there."

Luken nodded. "And we will, but the guards could return at any moment."

He was right, but as I wiped away my tears, I still couldn't move. Now that I'd found my parents, I didn't want to let them out of my sight. What if I never saw them again?

I wished I could at least make sure they were okay.

"Wait," I said, an idea blooming in my brain. "You're a fairy, which means you can do the creepy dream thing."

Luken let out a long sigh. "Technically yes, fairies are able to access dreams. But it is nothing I approve of. Our dreams should be our own."

"Please, I need to know if my parents are okay. Can you look into their dreams and see what's being done to them?" I glanced down the long corridor. "To everyone? Why are they all having the exact same dream?"

"But—"

"I'm not going anywhere unless I know they're not being hurt!"

Luken sighed again. "All right, I will do it. Then we must return to our rooms."

"Fine," I said.

He nodded and closed his eyes, a look of intense concentration sweeping over his face. Then he got totally still, like a statue, and stopped breathing for a moment. I stopped breathing too as I watched him.

After a couple minutes, his eyes opened again. "I have never felt anything like it before," he said. "They are there, and yet they are not."

"What does that mean?"

"It is…hard to explain. Their thoughts are active, but their dreams are being controlled by an outside force."

"But they're all right?"

"Yes," said Luken. He shook his head. "I do not understand. Fairies are able to see dreams, but they should never control them. To do so is barbaric!"

"Well, then you obviously don't know your people very well. Look around. Everyone here is having their dreams controlled."

"Why?" said Luken. "To what end?"

"You tell me," I said.

A voice boomed down the hallway, interrupting our conversation: "He shall do no such thing."

I spun around to see Mahlia and several fairy guards standing in the doorway. We'd been caught.

"Run!" I cried, grabbing Luken's hand.

With one last glance at my parents' motionless forms, I dragged Luken down the hallway away from Mahlia. I heard footsteps echo behind us, but that only made me run faster. I didn't know where we were going. We couldn't exactly sneak back into our rooms now and pretend nothing had happened. But I'd found my parents. That was the most important thing.

"Luken," I said, panting. "Are there any of your tunnels around here?"

"Yes," he said. "On the other side of the building. If we can just—"

He didn't get a chance to finish his thought. As we zipped around a corner, several figures appeared a few steps ahead of us. The Queen's Guard.

I put on the brakes and whirled around, hoping we could run back in the other direction. Unfortunately, another group of fairies was right behind us. Mahlia stood in the center, her long arms folded in front of her chest. For once, she wasn't smiling.

Instead, she held up her star-shaped wand and—

Zap!

A wave of energy hit my body, knocking me backward

onto the stone floor. I tried to scramble to my feet, but for some reason they weren't working like they should. They were too short. And there were four of them. And there was something else attached to me, something that didn't feel right at all.

When I glanced over my shoulder, I realized it was a tail. A long, thin, disgusting rodent tail.

I'd been moused.

PART II

Chapter Nineteen

I stared down at my mouse body in horror. Four legs. Light brown fur. And a tail! My poufy pink dress had shrunk along with me, which meant I looked like a little rodent ballerina. Perfect.

Once the initial shock wore off, I realized I needed to get out of here and fast. I tried to scamper away, unsteady on my short legs, but Mahlia cut me off and scooped me up in her pale hand. I spotted Luken towering nearby. Lucky for him, he'd avoided getting moused.

"Let me go!" I cried, my voice like a tiny, garbled harmonica.

As Mahlia cupped me in her hand, I ran my mouse tongue over my sharp mouse teeth. Then I opened my mouth and chomped down on her thumb, goblin-style.

"Ouch!" she cried, but she didn't let me go. Instead, she waved her wand again, and a tiny, gold cage materialized around me.

All at once, I noticed how incredibly itchy my nose was. I kept twitching it, but that didn't do any good. I guess that's what happened when you had whiskers sprouting out of your face.

"Let Jenny go," I heard Luken say.

"Impossible," Mahlia answered. "The queen will already be displeased that she was able to run off. We cannot have her escaping before her majesty has gotten what she wants."

"And what does she want, Mother? Why is she keeping Jenny and her parents here?"

My mouse ears perked up. Maybe I'd finally get some answers!

Mahlia just shook her head, sending white powder flying from her hair, and said, "It is not your concern." She waved her wand, and a new cuff materialized around Luken's wrist to replace the one he'd deactivated. "Now return to your room and do not let me catch you sneaking around again, or I will have no choice but to punish you."

"I thought you were doing all this to keep me safe," said Luken. "And now you are threatening me?"

"I *am* keeping you safe!" Mahlia cried. "The only way to make certain nothing happens to you is to do what the queen wants."

My Sort of Fairy Tale Ending

Luken was obviously done listening. He turned and stalked off, followed by two fairy guards.

I watched in amazement as Mahlia dabbed at tears in her eyes. I guess she really did care about her son, even if she was going about protecting him in the worst way possible.

As Mahlia took off down the hall, I struggled to find a way out of the tiny cage. I'd heard that mice could squeeze through impossibly small spaces, but when I tried to stick my head through the bars, it almost got stuck. So much for that idea. Worst of all, every time I moved around, my tail kept almost tripping me. How did real mice do it?

Finally, we got to a door that was just around the corner from the lab where I'd seen my parents. One of the fairy guards opened the door, and Mahlia brought me into what looked like a dimly lit storage room but smelled like a pet store. The gray walls were lined with gold cages, all filled with prisoners who'd been turned into mice and birds. I couldn't imagine what they'd all done to wind up here.

I expected Mahlia to put me into one of the bigger cages with some of the other mice. Instead, she placed my small cage by itself in the corner. She probably didn't want to take any chances that I'd find a way to escape.

Just before she left, Mahlia turned back to me and

sighed. "I am sorry," she said softly. Then she strode out of the room and locked the door behind her.

Okay. Now what?

"Anthony?" I called out. I was willing to bet the queen had quickly realized the gnome was not her true prince and had sent him here. I kept calling his name, but when I finally got an answer, it wasn't from Anthony.

"Jenny," a squeaky voice said from somewhere nearby.

I turned to see a mouse peering back at me from the next cage over, her gray nose twitching. Thanks to the mouse's sparkly, purple sweater, I knew right away that she was Ilda.

Perfect. The fairies had put me next to one of the most manipulative people I'd ever met on my adventures. Those aliens sure knew how to push my buttons.

"What do you want?" I squeaked back, hating the sound of my tiny voice.

"I was waiting for you to end up here," she said. "I'm glad you've finally come. I have something important to tell you."

"Something important, huh?" I was in no mood for Ilda's mind games. "Let me guess. You're going to tell me my parents are here."

The witch let out a chirping laugh. "That was part of it, but you seem to already know that."

"Then what?" I couldn't help being curious, despite myself. Even if Ilda had done nothing but lie to me when I'd first met her, she was also the reason I'd finally found out where to look for my mom and dad.

"Your parents," she said in a dramatic whisper, "are here in Fairy Land *willingly*."

I stared at her. "What do you mean?"

"They agreed to be kept here and used as part of the Queen Fairy's plan."

"No way. They would never help her."

"It's the truth, Jenny. The queen told me herself. After she snatched your parents from my land, she threatened to kidnap you too, if they refused to help her. They agreed to do whatever it took to keep you safe, even if it meant never seeing you again."

I wanted to tell myself she was lying. After all, Ilda loved saying things that upset me. Then again, she had no reason to lie now. She was trapped here just like I was.

Could it be true? Had my parents spent all these years trapped in Fairy Land because they'd been trying to protect me from that glowing psycho fairy? If they'd been willing to make that kind of deal with her, then they'd obviously had no idea how to defeat the queen.

I sank to the floor of my cage, feeling like something was pressing down on me. If my parents—the greatest adventurers in history—hadn't been able to bring down the Queen Fairy, then what chance did I have?

Chapter Twenty

The hours ticked by as I sat in my miniscule cage, totally out of ideas. In the morning, I'd be brought to the Queen Fairy to give her my answer. Not only was I no closer to rescuing my parents, but now I had to deal with a constant, overwhelming cheese craving.

I tried to focus on the comforting weight around my neck of my mother's necklace, which had shrunk down to mouse-size along with me, and let it soothe me. Hopefully, my mom's jewelry would go back to normal when I was human again. *If* I was ever human again.

Okay, this wasn't helping.

I was so on edge that I didn't think I'd be able to get even a minute of sleep, but after a while my eyelids started to droop. Great. The fairies were probably luring me into one of their creepy dreams again. I tried to fight it, but my eyes didn't listen to me. My lids got heavier and heavier until it felt like fingers were pressing them shut.

Finally, I stopped struggling, curled up in a tight ball, and let the dream take me away.

This time I was in the Land of Tales, outside of Princess Nartha's palace. Just like during my real mission, I was trying to convince the villagers that I was there to help them. *Un*like in my real mission, the Committee members suddenly materialized alongside Jasmine, another adventurer about my age. I expected the old women to scold me for breaking the rules—that's what they always did when I was around—but this time they surprised me by shaking their heads sadly and telling me they would understand if I betrayed them to save my parents. Even Jasmine, who was the most cautious and law-abiding person I'd ever met, agreed that getting my mom and dad back was the most important thing.

As if to prove just how serious they were, the Committee members snapped their fingers, and a signed and stamped form flew down from the sky with the words "Permission granted" written across it. Having the Committee members' blessing should have made me happy. Instead, I felt horrible for even thinking of betraying them. And sure enough, the prickle in the back of my brain was there again, stronger than ever.

"I want to wake up," I said, just like I'd done the first night. "Now." Once again, it worked.

I opened my eyes, my mind spinning. Even in my mouse state, the fairies had been controlling my dream, trying to tell me that turning over the Committee was my only choice. But that couldn't be true. There had to be another solution.

I sat up, wide awake, an idea bouncing around in my tiny mouse brain. Maybe there was a way I could get my parents back *and* keep the Committee safe. And get rid of that glowing faux-Cinderella once and for all.

• • •

What felt like days (but was only hours) later, Mahlia and her fairy guards appeared in the storage room. The animals around me erupted in squeaks and chirps, desperate to be let out. Mahlia ignored all of them and came straight over to me. Then she picked up my cage and brought me to the elevator so we could ride to the top floor.

The whole way up, as the fairies screamed, my furry body shivered with excitement while my nose itched even worse than before. My plan had to work. It just had to.

When I got to the Queen Fairy's throne room, I noticed she'd dressed it up since the last time I'd been here. The whole place sparkled like a gaudy chandelier. The Queen Fairy stepped forward, looking like she could generate electricity. I shuddered to think what her touch might feel like.

Mahlia placed my cage directly in front of the throne, and then she and her guards left the room.

It was only then that I noticed another smaller throne had been placed next to the queen's. And on that throne, surrounded by towers of candy, was none other than Anthony.

What on earth? I'd thought Anthony was being kept prisoner somewhere, and instead he was here stuffing himself with candy and pretending to be a ruler?

The gnome didn't notice me as he shoveled handful after handful of sugary treats into his mouth so fast that the small crown on his head was shaking. He was now wearing two glass loafers. The queen must have decided he was her true prince, after all.

It was only when the queen stood up and said, "Jenny the Adventurer," that Anthony stopped eating and looked up.

"Jenny-girl, is that you?" He giggled. "The mouse look suits you almost as much as the royal look suits me."

I couldn't believe it. Was he really going to ignore everything the queen had done just because she'd given him all the candy he could want? Didn't he care that she'd taken my parents and imprisoned tons of people? And that thanks to the fairies, I now had a *tail*?

"Anthony, what are you doing?" I demanded.

As he grinned back at me, I noticed that his eyes were weirdly glazed over. Either the queen had put some kind of spell on him or he'd had so much sugar that it had sent his brain into overload. "I know it seems hasty, Jenny-girl, but I'm getting married! The wedding's tomorrow. I'm sure you're invited. Imagine, after all these years of being just a magical guide, I finally get to be the one giving orders!"

"My dear," the Queen Fairy said to Anthony in a sickeningly sweet voice, "remember what we talked about. You must stay quiet while I conduct my business."

"Oh, right," he said. "Sorry, pookie." Then he went back to popping candy in his mouth.

"Now, Jenny," said the queen. "Your three days are up. Have you made a decision?"

"Yup," I squeaked in reply. "My answer is yes. I'll do it. I'll help you get to the Committee."

"Excellent," she said immediately, like she'd known all along that I'd agree to her proposal. "Tell me their location."

"I don't know their location. How many times do I have to tell you that?"

"If that is true, then you have nothing to trade." The Queen Fairy raised her hand like she was going to summon her guards.

"No, wait! Just because I don't know where the Committee is, that doesn't mean I don't have a way to get there."

"Explain."

"Anthony can send me."

The gnome stopped licking the armrest of his throne—which was apparently also made out of candy—and his glazed-over eyes focused on me. "Wait, what?" he said.

The Queen Fairy's smile dimmed. "Darling," she said to Anthony, "you did not tell me you could bring me to the Committee."

He shrugged. "You never asked. Besides, I still have this on, remember?" He held up the orange cuff that was blocking him from using his magic.

The queen turned to me. "Our deal is off. If my fiancé can take me, then I do not need your help."

Uh-oh. This wasn't how the plan was supposed to go. "But—but if you send me to the Committee members first, I'll talk them into surrendering to you. Then you won't even have to fight them. Think of all the magic you'll save!"

She laughed. "Do you really think I am a fool? I will not simply release you."

"Of course not," I said. "I'll have a cuff on, remember? You'll know exactly where I am."

As the queen seemed to consider what I'd said, I had to stop my brain from running through all the things that could go wrong with my plan. What if Anthony sent me to the Committee and the members didn't listen to me? What if I couldn't convince the old women to take my cuff off right away and the Queen Fairy managed to track us down? What if this was the absolute worst plan I'd ever come up with?

Shut up, brain! This plan had to work or I was totally out of options.

Finally, the Queen Fairy stood up. "Very well."

Score!

"Jenny-girl," Anthony said, "you know I'd do anything for your parents, but are you sure about this?" Maybe he hadn't completely lost his mind, after all.

"I'm sure," I said, hoping that through his sugar haze, he could tell this was all part of my plan. I turned back to the queen. "Before we do anything, how about turning me back into a human? If I go off to the Committee like this, someone might step on me and mess up everything."

The queen sighed. Then she waved her hand and—*zap*!

My legs got longer and longer, my body larger and larger, and my skin less and less furry, until...I was me again!

"*Achoo!*" An unbelievably satisfying sneeze exploded out of me. Finally, the itching in my nose stopped.

"All right," said the queen. "Now go."

"Wait." I had to find a way to whisper my plan to Anthony first. "I just want to—"

"No," she said. "I am tired of waiting. If you do not go now, our deal is off."

Before I could say anything else, a deafening *Pop!* filled the throne room.

I whirled around, hoping to see a Committee-led army coming to rescue us. Instead, there was only a sole figure in the middle of the room, holding a wooden cane instead of a weapon.

Dr. Bradley.

Chapter Twenty-One

"Welcome back, Doc!" Anthony called out. "Where have you been hiding all this time?"

Dr. Bradley didn't answer. Instead, he hobbled toward the Queen Fairy. "Release them," he hissed. I'd never heard him sound so threatening.

Not surprisingly, the Queen Fairy ignored him. She whispered some sort of command, and instantly I heard footsteps coming down the hallway.

"Get us out of here!" I cried to Dr. Bradley. If he'd managed to transport himself here, that meant he could pop us back out. Once we regrouped, we'd figure out how to get my parents out too.

Dr. Bradley raised his cane just as the Queen Fairy started shooting waves of energy at him. He managed to deflect one—two—three waves and send them crashing into the floor. Meanwhile, I yanked Anthony off his throne and dragged him toward the doctor, so the three of us could get into world-jumping position.

"Hey, what are you doing?" said Anthony. He tried to grab handfuls of candy as I dragged him away.

As my fingers were about to wrap around the doctor's elbow, another beam of energy hit and knocked Dr. Bradley's cane across the room.

"No!" the doctor cried. He tried deflecting more of the queen's attacks with his own magic, but it was too weak. I watched, helpless, as the doctor fell to the ground.

Just then, a wave of energy slammed into me. *Zap!*

And just like that, I was shrinking all over again and sprouting extra legs, a tail, and fur. This was ridiculous! How many times was I going to get moused and unmoused in the span of an hour? Beside me, the doctor and Anthony were also morphing into woodland creatures. I noticed that one of Dr. Bradley's small paws had an orange cuff around it. Now his magic was useless too.

Before any of us could scamper away, a cage appeared around all three of us. We were trapped.

"Take them away," I heard the Queen Fairy say.

"Hey!" Anthony squeaked as a guard picked up our cage. "What are you doing? I'm the queen's future husband."

"Do not worry, my dear," said the queen. "I will retrieve you in time for the wedding. And after that, you will have your very own cage."

Anthony's eyes bugged out. He seemed to be finally coming out of his sugar haze. Maybe learning that the queen intended to keep him as a pet was enough to sober him up.

"Wait!" I cried. "What about my parents? What about our deal?"

The Queen Fairy didn't answer. Instead, she disappeared behind one of the hanging tapestries, like the sun setting behind a cloud. I guess that meant any hope of making a deal was gone.

"I can't believe it," said Anthony as the guards carried our cage down the hall. "She gave me all the candy I could ever want. She said I was the one she'd been waiting for and she'd do anything to make me happy. She even convinced me wear these uncomfortable shoes!" He kicked his tiny glass loafers off his furry feet so they landed on the floor of the cage. "And now she's turned me into a disgusting creature and locked me up?"

"What did you expect?" I said.

Anthony sighed. "I guess you're right. It was too good

to be true. But the throne…it tasted so good!" His eyes started to glaze over again. "Maybe if I go apologize to the queen, she'll let me—"

I smacked him with my tail. "Snap out of it!"

Anthony's mouse eyes focused back on me. "You're right. It's over. The candy throne is gone." He turned to Dr. Bradley. "Where have you been all this time, Doc? And why couldn't you find anyone to help break us out of here?"

"I pleaded with the Committee to organize an effort to rescue you," said the doctor, peering down at his four legs. Just like when he was human, one of them was made out of metal. I wasn't sure how he'd be able to move around without his cane, but maybe having three good legs would help. "Alas," he went on, "they deliberated for days about what to do, but in the end—"

"Let me guess," I said. "They told you the mission was too dangerous and they'd have to study the matter further."

He sighed. "Something like that."

I wanted to laugh. It figured that I'd spent all this time trying to think of ways to keep the Committee safe from the fairies, and they didn't even care that the Queen Fairy had trapped us here forever. What was the point of staying loyal to those grumpy old ladies when they were willing to just let us rot here?

I twitched my whiskers. Well, it was too late now. Even if I decided to give up the Committee for real, the Queen Fairy wasn't interested in making a deal anymore.

The guards brought us into the elevator, and we shot down through what seemed like about a million levels. Anthony and I automatically put our front paws up and shrieked along with the guards. Dr. Bradley stared at both of us as if we'd gone totally insane. Maybe we had.

Finally, we emerged in the lower level where the other prisoners were being kept. And where my parents were probably still asleep in the lab. What would they think if they found out their daughter had been turned into a mouse, not once but twice? I suspected they'd be disappointed in me, and probably a little grossed out that their only child now had fur growing out of her ears.

The guards put our cage right next to Ilda's before leaving and closing the door behind them. The witch scurried over as if she was excited to see me.

"Back so soon? Did you make a deal with the queen?"

I sighed. "Nope. I guess it's time for Plan B."

"What's Plan B?" said Anthony.

"I don't know yet, but we have to find some way to get out of here."

A voice chimed in from the cage on the other side of us: "Don't bother. There's no escape."

I glanced over to see a small mouse in a leprechaun outfit curled into a little ball in the corner. Something clicked in my head. "Are you Belthum?" I said.

The mouse blinked at me, obviously startled. "Yes. How did you know?"

"Your father's been so worried about you!" I said.

Before I could tell him about Karfum's plan to fight against the queen, the door to the chamber creaked open. Were the fairy guards coming back to turn us into snakes this time? Or worse, were they going to make us sing?

I peered through the bars of my cage and spotted someone tiptoeing toward us. It was Luken.

"Jenny?" he called softly. "Are you there?"

I squeaked and waved him over with my front paws. "What are you doing here?"

He crouched by our cage and whispered, "I came as soon as I could deactivate the new cuff. They made this one even more difficult than the last."

"Luken?" said Belthum, his voice full of disbelief as he came to the bars of his cage. "Is that you?"

"Belthum, my friend," said Luken, looking downright joyful. "I knew I would see you again. I just knew it!"

I hated to interrupt the happy reunion, but we had to get out of here as soon as possible. "Luken, can you use your magic to break us out of this cage?" Since there was no door or lock, magic had to be the only way.

He shook his head. "I cannot use the magic. I *will* not."

"Why not? You deactivated your cuff, didn't you? That means they're not tracking your magic anymore."

"I want to help you. Really." Luken's thin shoulders sagged. "You must know, Jenny, that I have never agreed with what my people do. Even when I was a young child, I could not understand how they could teach me that stealing is immoral and yet do it themselves."

"Stealing magic," I said. "Yeah, the fairies like doing that. I don't know why they bother when they already have plenty."

Luken's eyes were full of sadness. "You misunderstand. The fairies do not steal magic out of greed. They steal it out of necessity. If the fairies do not take magic, then they have none of their own. They are powerless."

Chapter Twenty-Two

"What are you talking about?" I said. "Fairies have tons of magic. I mean, look at us! Do you think we turned *ourselves* into four-legged creatures?"

Luken shook his head. "Fairies can read dreams, but that is the extent of their natural magic. Before the Queen Fairy took over this land, my people used their abilities to make the amusement park exactly what visitors wanted. It was only when the Queen Fairy devised a way to take magic from others that she remade this land into her own fairy-tale kingdom."

I thought of the Land of Tales and how its residents had lost their way of life because their magic was gone. The Queen Fairy had destroyed their world in order to keep her own running.

No wonder all that glowing magic was practically bursting out of her. She wasn't supposed to have it in the first place. I wouldn't be surprised if she actually sweated magic. (Did fairies sweat? Something told me they probably didn't.)

"Okay, so fairies steal magic. What does that have to do with adventurers?" I said. "Why does the queen have them in that lab?"

Luken put his head in his hands. "You must believe that I did not know what she was doing to your parents until I finally got the truth out of my mother today."

"What?" I said, sticking my long nose through the bars. "What is it?"

"The Queen Fairy discovered that adventurers are extremely valuable. They magnify and focus magic so it is more useful to her."

"You mean my parents and the other adventurers are being used liked they're magnifying glasses? That doesn't make sense. My mom and dad aren't even magical."

Luken shook his head. "Being magical does not matter. Adventurers spend their lives putting the magical worlds in order. That is why they are so effective in focusing magic once the Queen Fairy has taken it. After the magic is absorbed, they help send it out to the fairies through the red cuffs."

That's why the fairies had been so interested when they'd found out I was an adventurer. I thought of the way my dreams had been repeats of some of my missions. Maybe the fairies had been testing me to see if I was a good fit for their magic-channeling purposes. Hopefully, I'd been a miserable failure.

"So you won't use the magic, even if it'll help us?" I asked Luken.

"I cannot, Jenny. When I first decided to stand up to the queen, I swore I would not use stolen magic again. My father would have never approved."

I was tempted to try to talk Luken into it anyway, but I couldn't force him to do something he thought was so wrong. "Okay, do you have any other ideas on how we can get out of here?"

Luken smiled. "In fact, I think I do," he said. "The key is the lab. The queen is able to keep the city running because the adventurers focus the magic as it flows into the cuffs. But if all the adventurers were to wake up at once—"

"Instead of going into the cuffs, the magic would go all over the place!" I had to admit the plan was pretty brilliant. "And the magic keeping us in here would disappear too, right?"

Luken nodded. "Or at least be weakened significantly. Once the magic has been disrupted, you will be able to escape. You may even turn back to your regular forms."

"What about me?" said Ilda, her eyes wide with panic. "You'll help me escape too, won't you?"

I sighed. As tempting as it was, I couldn't leave the old harpy behind. "Yeah, we'll take you with us. In fact, we'll make sure to get all the prisoners out." *Somehow*, I added silently.

Dr. Bradley had been quietly listening until now, but he finally chimed in. "Do you know how you will wake up the adventurers?"

"I am still working out that part of the plan," Luken admitted. "There must be some way to interrupt the magic that is keeping them asleep."

My brain started churning. Luken was right. There had to be a way to get my parents and the other adventurers out of their comas. After all, I'd managed to wake myself up when the fairies were trying to control my dreams.

Ding! That was it!

"I might have the answer," I said. "When the fairies were messing with my dreams, I just had to say that I wanted to wake up, and somehow it worked." I turned to Luken. "Once you sneak into the lab, you can go from person to person, tap into their dreams, and tell them to wake themselves up."

"It will not be easy," he said, rubbing his ear. "I imagine it will require quite a bit of my energy."

"You'll be able to do it, right? If you can't, then I don't know if there's another way."

Luken nodded, a determined look on his face. "Yes. I will do it. No matter what."

"But, Luken," said Belthum, not sounding convinced, "how will you get into the lab in the first place? It's always guarded."

"I will persuade Karfum to help distract the fairy guards."

Belthum shook his head. "You know my father won't help. He disapproves of our rebellion."

"You might be surprised," I said, remembering Karfum's tearful breakdown in the elevator. As I turned back to Luken, hope warmed my body like sunlight. Maybe we could really pull this off. "How soon can you get everything going?"

Luken sighed. "I wish we could do it now, but it will have to be tomorrow morning. That will give me time to make certain everything is ready. I only hope the queen does not change her mind and put you in the lab before then."

I shuddered. "Why didn't she put me there in the first place? Doesn't she want to use my magic-magnifying skills?"

"I believe she still thinks she might be able to reason with you," said Luken. "According to my mother, the Committee members are the only ones with enough power to stop the queen. I think the Queen Fairy is afraid of what might happen if they get to her first."

Wow, the queen really had to be afraid of the Committee to want to try to make another deal with me. Maybe she wasn't as powerful as I'd thought. Or those annoying Committee members were more magical than I'd been giving them credit for.

"Okay, then it's settled," I said. "Tomorrow, we finally get out of here."

Chapter Twenty-Three

The hours crept by as I lay curled up in the corner of the cage, trying not to explode from impatience. Everyone around me was sleeping, including Anthony, whose snores were so loud that I'd never believe the saying "quiet as a mouse" again.

Eventually, I focused on a game in my mind that I hadn't let myself play in a while: what life will be like once I get my parents back.

I imagined finally bringing my parents home and the whole town having a welcome-back party for them. Then the three of us, plus Aunt Evie, would go play mini-golf. We'd have such a great time that my parents would decide to *buy* the mini-golf course so we could live there if we wanted. Then my parents would tell me that they would never leave me again, and that I could stop going to school so that I could spend more time with them. And then they'd say, "What do you think, Jenny? Jenny? Jenny!"

My eyes popped open. I must have finally dozed off.

"Jenny!" I realized Anthony was the one saying my name over and over.

"What?"

"Look!" He and Dr. Bradley were staring at the bars of the cage which were now glowing. This had to be a sign from Luken.

"It's time," I said.

We waited. And waited some more. Just when I was starting to wonder if the glowing wasn't a sign after all, something in the air shifted and my ears popped. Then, the tops of all the golden cages started melting.

"He did it!" I jumped to my feet, ready to run the minute enough of the cage had melted. The other prisoners and I tried to protect ourselves as globs of hot metal dripped down on our furry bodies.

But as quickly as the bars had started melting, they stopped. The cages were still mostly intact, and the metal continued to glow red hot. I couldn't even touch the bars without risking getting burned.

"So much for that plan," said Ilda, flopping back onto the floor of her cage.

I wasn't about to give up that easily. "Something must

have gone wrong," I said. "At least the cages are weaker now. That means we might be able to escape."

Anthony stood next to me, peering up at the top of the cage that had melted all the way through. "If only we had some climbing gear so we could get up to the top," he said. "Oh wait. We *did* have climbing gear, but *someone* made me get rid of it."

Instead of pointing out that mice weren't exactly known for their rock-climbing skills, I ignored him and kept racking my brain for a plan. Finally, I wrapped the skirt of my poufy dress around my paws and pushed on one of the bars of my cage. The fabric let out a soft *hiss*, and I had to pull my paws away after a second. But where I'd touched it, the metal bar was now slightly dented.

"Look, everybody!" I cried. "The bars are still soft. We might be able to pry them apart! Just be careful. They're really hot."

The cages around us erupted in a frenzy of activity as everyone grabbed pieces of clothing for protection and started tugging and pushing on the bars.

Anthony and I worked furiously to get the bars of our cage far enough apart that one of us could climb through. Finally, the opening was just wide enough for me.

"Go, find Luken and your parents," said Dr. Bradley, coming to take my place. "Anthony and I will keep going."

"I can't go yet. I need to help all the other animals escape!"

"Nonsense," said Ilda, as she pulled on the bars of her own cage. "You must learn when to delegate tasks. Free your parents. We'll do the rest."

"Go, Jenny-girl," said Anthony. "We'll be fine."

I nodded. "Okay, I'll find Luken, and then we'll come back for you guys."

I scampered toward the door of the storage room, hoping to be able to push it open. But even if it had been unlocked, it was far too heavy for me to move. The only option was the gap under the door. It was thin—almost as narrow as the bars on the cage had been—but there was no choice. I had to get through.

I took a deep breath and then got on my belly. After shoving my nose and face under the door, I crawled and wriggled until it felt like I was being fed through a pasta-maker. Finally, I oozed out on the other side of the door like a layer of Play-Doh.

Without stopping to catch my breath, I dashed down the hall toward the door to the lab. When I got to the door, I found it unguarded this time. Luken must have convinced Karfum to help him distract the fairy guards somehow.

Once again, I had to squeeze under the door. This time I barely even noticed how uncomfortable it was. All I cared about was that my parents were waiting for me on the other side.

When I emerged inside the lab, I could feel the magic humming through the room. It was weaker than the last time I'd been here, but not by much.

As I sprinted down the corridor, I spotted someone sprawled on the floor right in front of my parents' cell. Oh no.

"Luken!" I cried.

Chapter Twenty-Four

"Luken!" I said, nipping at him with my teeth since my paws were far too small to shake him with. "Luken, wake up!"

He didn't look injured and he was still breathing, but he wouldn't open his eyes. I couldn't figure out what was wrong. Maybe trying to go into so many people's dreams had been too much for him to handle.

My tiny mouse heart was beating so fast that I was afraid it might punch through my furry chest. I had to do something. When I glanced around, I realized that some of the prisoners in the cells were awake. They looked groggy and disoriented, like they had no idea where they were, but they were coming out of their comas.

Hesitantly, I peered into my parents' cell, and my heart went from beating too hard to not beating at all.

They were awake. Both of them. And they were staring back at me.

"Mom! Dad!" I cried. "Are you okay?"

They peered at me with confused eyes. Maybe they couldn't hear me through the glass. Or they couldn't figure out why a mouse was convinced they were its parents.

I tore my gaze away from them as Luken finally began to stir. His eyes opened slowly, and he looked down at me.

"Jenny," he said. "I am sorry. I did what I could…"

"You did great," I assured him. "I got out of my cage, and a bunch of the adventurers are waking up. My parents are awake!"

"It was not enough…"

"You gave us an opening. We'll figure out the rest."

"What…what is happening to you?" he said, his eyes widening.

"What do you mean?" I realized that my voice didn't sound as squeaky as before. I glanced down and saw that my front paws were starting to look more and more like human hands. "I'm turning back!"

My body started growing faster and faster. I waited for the magic to return me to my normal form, but suddenly it stopped. I was horrified to realize that I still had a very long and very gross tail attached to my otherwise human body.

"What happened?" I said.

"Waking the adventurers must not have been enough," said Luken as I helped him sit up. Tail or not, I was itching to go talk to my parents, but I wanted to stay with him to make sure he was okay.

"Go see them," he said, as if he could read my mind. "I will be fine."

"But—"

"Jenny, really." He got to his feet, as if to prove just how fine he was. "I am all right. Tell me what I can do and then go to your parents."

There was no arguing with Luken. He was as stubborn as I was.

"Fine," I said. "Go back to the storage room and make sure everyone's out of their cages. I'll meet you there."

Luken nodded and hurried away. He wasn't moving as gracefully as usual, but he seemed okay.

When he was gone, I rushed over to my parents' cell. I could feel the energy pulsing across the door, but it was much weaker now. As more and more adventurers woke up, the magic became less and less focused. Maybe once they were all out of their comas, the fairies would lose total control of the magic. Then we could leave Fairy Land without a problem. And my horrible extra appendage would disappear.

"Mom. Dad," I said, going over to the glass. They turned to look at me, which meant they could hear me, after all. "I'm going to get you out, okay? But I need your help."

They stared at me, still dazed.

"The cots," I said, pointing to their narrow beds. "Can you push them into the door? If we can get it open a crack, I can pull it from the other side."

My parents shared a glance and then nodded. They grabbed the beds, exchanged whispers, and then rammed the cots into the door at the same time. It didn't budge.

"I'm sorry," my dad said, his voice muffled behind the glass. "We're very weak."

I almost burst into tears on the spot. My dad's voice was exactly like I remembered it. It was him. It was really him!

But I couldn't lose it now. I had to get my parents out. "Try one more time," I said.

My parents nodded. This time, they both grabbed on to one of the cots and pushed it together. They ran at the door and—*bang*! The cot slammed into the glass door and forced it open just enough for me to be able to grab on to it.

I whooped with excitement.

"Okay, hold on," I told my parents. "I'm coming to get you!"

If I waited, maybe the magic would be weak enough that I wouldn't have to fight through any energy fields, but I wasn't going to risk waiting another second. Not when I had this chance to finally get to my parents.

"One, two, three," I muttered. Then I grabbed the edge of the glass door and pulled as hard as I could. A wave of energy flowed through my body, but I barely noticed it. All I could think about was the fact that my parents were less than two feet away from me. No stupid door was going to stand in my way, no matter how much it tried to electrocute me.

With one last yank, the door flew open, and I was thrown backward. It took me a second to scramble to my feet, but then there was no stopping me.

"Mom! Dad!" I cried, rushing into the cell. I threw my arms around my parents, tears streaming down my face. I didn't care that I was sobbing. All I cared about was that I'd done it. I'd found them.

It took me a minute to realize that my parents weren't really hugging me back. Instead, they were peering back at me in total confusion.

"What's wrong?" I said. "Are you guys okay? Aren't you happy to see me?"

My parents looked at each other. Then they looked at me.

"I'm sorry," my mom said, "but do we know you?"

Chapter Twenty-Five

"I'm Jenny, your daughter. You—you left me seven years ago, and I've been looking for you. I found you. I'm here. I look different now because I'm older, and I have a tail. The tail's only temporary, though. At least, I hope it is. But I'm your daughter. I'm Jenny."

As I babbled on, I kept waiting for my parents to tell me they were joking, that they knew who I was after all. They only shook their heads sadly.

"We've been through quite an ordeal," my dad said. "It must have affected our brains. To be honest, I don't remember much of anything." He thought for a second. "In fact, I'm not sure I know my own name."

My mother nodded. "Whatever the fairies did to us, it had an impact on our memories."

My jaw started shaking like I'd been out in the freezing cold for too long. I couldn't believe it. My parents were talking like we were strangers. How could they not know me? I was their daughter!

"You remember the fairies, but you don't remember me?" I said, my voice quivering. Even my tail was shaking.

My mom gave me a sad smile. "I'm sure we will, in time. It's probably temporary."

"Now, you said you're here to rescue us?" said my dad.

I took in a long breath. Right. The mission. My parents might not remember me, but it was still my job to get them out of here and home safely. I'd deal with the rest later.

"Okay," I said, swallowing the tears in my throat. "We have to get the rest of these cells open, and then we need to find my friends."

My parents nodded. Even though they were still obviously weak and disoriented, their adventurer instincts must have kicked in because they got to work right away. Together, we went through the lab and freed the rest of the prisoners. Luckily, the magic was fading fast, so most of the cell doors were barely electrified anymore.

"Bless you," an older woman about Dr. Bradley's age said when I let her out of her cell. "I thought I would be trapped in those horrid dreams forever." Then she surprised me by pulling me into a warm hug. I couldn't help wishing that my parents had hugged me like that when I'd found them.

No. I wouldn't think about that now. *Focus on the mission, Jenny*, I told myself. *Get everyone home.*

When the last of the prisoners in the lab were free, I realized everyone was looking to me for instructions. Most of the prisoners were adventurers, but they were all still dazed and weak. It was up to me to figure out what to do.

First off, I had to get back to the storage room and meet up with Luken and the rest of my friends. Bringing all the adventurers with me wasn't the best idea, but I didn't know what else to do with them.

"Follow me," I said, heading down the hallway. Behind me, a snake of people dressed in stiff hospital gowns followed. We would have made a pretty depressing parade.

We didn't see any sign of fairies or leprechaun guards. Something about this whole thing felt too easy, but I tried to shake that thought out of my head. I'd nearly burned and electrocuted myself; that wasn't exactly *easy*.

As we walked along the corridors, I noticed that the gray stone walls were starting to look faded. In a couple of spots, the walls had bright colors bleeding through.

"What's happening here?" one of the prisoners asked as

the hallway we were trudging down started to morph into a hall of mirrors.

"I think the theme park is coming back now that the queen's magic is fading," I said. I hoped that meant that one day the amusement park would come back completely, just like it had been before the queen took over the land.

When we got to the storage room, I couldn't help laughing at what I saw. Luken and Belthum were wrenching open the last of the cages while Anthony stood in the middle of the hallway entertaining people with some truly terrible juggling. Meanwhile, Dr. Bradley was making sure everyone was all right, and Ilda was putting everyone in orderly lines, probably the way she'd done back in her teaching days.

Like me, the creatures were mostly back to their usual forms, with some glaring exceptions. Anthony looked like an average gnome again except for the big, round ears on the top of his head; Ilda had a long snout and whiskers; and Dr. Bradley had an extra leg that made him look like a tripod.

When Dr. Bradley and Anthony spotted my parents, they both stopped what they were doing and rushed over.

"Finally!" Anthony said, throwing his arms around my mom and dad. "It's been way too long."

My Sort of Fairy Tale Ending

Dr. Bradley was beaming. "It is so good to see you, my friends," he said, once Anthony had released them.

My parents smiled weakly, obviously perplexed.

"They have amnesia," I explained. "They don't remember anyone. Not even..." I cleared my throat. "Not even me."

"Oh my," said Dr. Bradley. "That is unfortunate."

Anthony gave my elbow a sympathetic squeeze. "Their memories will come back. Magic messes with people, but usually they come out okay."

My brain fixed on that word: *usually*. I didn't care what usually happened. I wanted my parents to be okay right now. But what could I do?

"All right," I said. "Now that everyone's been freed, we have to find a way out of here."

Just then, the door to the storage room crashed open all by itself, like it had been pushed by a huge gust of wind. Then a blinding glow filled the room, and the Queen Fairy appeared, shining just as brightly as she had before. And she wasn't alone. An entire army of fairies stood behind her.

We were trapped.

Chapter Twenty-Six

"What do we do, Jenny-girl?" said Anthony.

"We fight," I said. "What else can we do?"

"Negotiate," said Luken. "I will make my mother listen to me."

I doubted that would work, but it was worth a try. Not all the fairies were magic-hungry monsters, after all. Luken had proven that.

As everyone else stared at the army of fairies, frozen, Luken went over to Mahlia.

"Mother, please," I heard him say. "We do not want to fight. We only want what is fair."

Mahlia appeared at a loss for words as she looked between her son and the queen. Maybe there *was* a chance we could reason with the fairies.

"There will be no negotiation," the Queen Fairy announced.

Or maybe not.

"Sweetness," said Anthony, stepping forward. "Please, consider what you're doing."

The queen ignored him. Clearly, she was done thinking she needed a prince by her side. "The leprechaun uprising has been contained," she went on, glaring at me. "You no longer have any allies here. Surrender to us." She didn't sound anything like Cinderella anymore. Now she was one hundred percent evil stepmother.

I swallowed, thinking of Karfum and the other leprechauns. Whatever the queen meant by "contained," it couldn't be good.

"Or what?" I said, going to stand beside Luken. "We woke up all your precious magic magnifiers. You might still be glowing, but you don't have all your power."

The queen let out a hollow laugh. "That is nothing to me. I have consumed nearly all the magic in existence. I am still powerful enough to dispose of all of you."

I had a feeling she wasn't exaggerating. Our plan might have worked to weaken the magic, but it hadn't been nearly enough to bring her down.

A murmur passed through the fairy army. The soldiers were staring at the Queen Fairy with wide eyes. For most of them, this was probably the first time they'd ever seen her. And there she was, glowing with power, admitting that she'd kept most of the stolen magic for herself instead of giving it to her people.

Just then, the citywide intercom went off. *Bing!* "*A reminder*," the overly cheerful voice said, "*that the weekly parade is about to begin. Attendance is mandatory. Enjoy!*"

The intercom fell silent, and the fairies shifted uncomfortably. They were so used to obeying all the intercom instructions that they obviously had no idea what to do.

Hmmm. Maybe the parade could be my chance to show everyone exactly what the queen had been up to.

"Luken," I whispered. "I need you to transport me to the parade."

He stared at me, his eyes full of disbelief. "But, Jenny—"

"Please!" I hissed. "Use the magic just this once. Even if it's stolen, it's the only way. We won't have another chance."

He still didn't look convinced.

"I know you're afraid you'll wind up like the other fairies," I continued in a whisper. "But you're not like them. You want to make things right, and so do I. The only way we can do that is to pop out of here and go up to that parade!"

"Luken!" Mahlia called. "Step away from that adventurer and come here."

He looked between me and his mother. Then he closed his eyes, grabbed my hand, and—*pop!*—we were out of there.

After a moment of mind-numbing spinning, we emerged in the middle of Main Street just as the parade was starting. It was a shock to be outside again, away from the queen. Everything around us was too bright and sharp, like I was seeing it through too-strong glasses.

Grinning fairies lined the street as floats went by at molasses speed. I'd expected the floats to be filled with waving fairies, but they were totally deserted. One was just a platform that was magically spewing bubbles into the air. Another was violently shooting glitter toward the sidewalk, into the spectators' faces. I had never seen bubbles and glitter look so un-festive. No wonder the Queen Fairy had to force everyone to come to the parades. There was nothing fun about them. On one of the palace walls, the parade was being broadcast for everyone to see.

A float shaped like Cinderella's carriage rolled past and everyone around us bowed. Unlike the pumpkin-shaped taxis, this one was much larger and had glitter-covered windows so it was impossible to see inside. No doubt this was the float the Queen Fairy used to travel around the land without anyone seeing how much power she'd stolen for herself.

"Now what?" said Luken. "It will not take long for the queen to find us."

As I watched an image of the carriage broadcast on the palace wall, I realized that the screen was showing a spot near us.

"Come on!" I said, pulling him toward the center of the street.

Just as we got there, a loud *Pop!* echoed around us. I didn't need to turn around to see who had appeared. I could feel the queen's magic bouncing off my skin.

"Enough of this!" the Queen Fairy said.

When I spun around, I saw that Mahlia had also appeared with my parents by her side. My mom and dad still looked disoriented, but at least they weren't hurt.

I took a deep breath and stepped up to face the queen. "Look at you," I said loudly. "You take all the magic for yourself and make everyone ration theirs. You're practically exploding with magic, and yet you tell everyone that there's not enough to go around. You take away all the fairy traditions and lock your people away in factories, while you sit around eating magic like it's popcorn!"

A wave of whispers passed through the crowd around us, and the queen's eyes shot up to the screen. There, on the side of the palace, the queen's glowing head was displayed for everyone to see, and they'd just heard every word that I'd said.

For once, the fairies were getting a good, long look at their queen. Maybe now they'd finally realize just what kind of leader she was.

"That cannot be the queen!" someone called. "Her carriage just passed by."

"Um, hello," I called back. "The carriage was empty. *This* is the real queen. I mean, look at her! Seeing is believing, right?"

The whispers were more furious this time. Maybe one of my cheesy sayings had finally done the trick.

"Silence," the queen said, raising a glowing hand. The fairies obeyed. "All I have done has been for you, my people. Never forget that." She turned back to me. "Now let us stop this foolishness. I have been more than patient with you, and my offer still stands. If you lead me to the Committee's location, I shall let you and your parents go free."

I glanced at my parents, who were watching the whole scene with confused eyes. I couldn't let the queen put them right back into that lab, not after I'd just found them. I couldn't! And yet...

"What about everyone else?" I said. "You need to let everyone in the Magical Village go back to their worlds and give the leprechauns back their pots of gold."

"Done," the queen said. "They are nothing to me."

"And release all the adventurers," I went on. "They're not your batteries. You can't just use them whenever you feel like it."

The Queen Fairy seemed to think this over. "Very well. Once I have the Committee's power, I will no longer need all those specimens. Even without them, I will be the most powerful entity in the magical kingdoms. And then my *true* prince and I will rule them together." Clearly, she didn't mean Anthony.

I thought of the dozens of creatures who had been imprisoned here for years. Even if the queen freed all the prisoners, what was to stop her from going to another world and enslaving everyone just like she'd done with the leprechauns? The Committee was the only group that had any chance of stopping her from doing that kind of thing again. If the Committee was gone, then the Queen Fairy could do whatever she wanted.

"Decide," said the queen. "Decide now or your chance is over. I will not let anything stand in the way of my happy ending!"

My breath caught in my throat. Hearing the queen echo the same words that I'd thought to myself so many times—how I needed, wanted, *deserved* a happily-ever-after—was like a slap in the face. Was I just as horrible as she was?

No. I wasn't. The Queen Fairy was willing to sacrifice all of the magical worlds for her happy ending. But I could never do something like that.

Even if it meant giving up on the one dream I'd had for so much of my life.

Even if it meant losing my family forever.

"Fine," I said, closing my eyes to keep tears from escaping. "I'll make a deal with you."

"Jenny!" Luken cried. "No!"

But I'd made up my mind. "You can have my parents."

Chapter Twenty-Seven

Everyone, including the Queen Fairy, stared at me in shock.

I felt like my head was underwater. I'd always thought I'd do whatever it took to bring my family back together. But not this.

"I'm an adventurer, just like my parents," I said. "I know they would never want me to make a deal that hurt anyone. I know they'd rather die than see the magical worlds destroyed. And I would rather die than do anything to make them ashamed of me."

"You would rather die?" the Queen Fairy screamed. "Then die!" She held up a glowing hand, aimed right at my chest. I didn't even have time to jump out of the way.

As I saw the beam of glowing energy shooting at me, I felt strangely calm. All I could think was that even if I never got to hear them say it, I knew my parents would be proud of me for putting the magical worlds first. Just like an adventurer was supposed to do.

As the beam was about to hit, I felt someone shove me out of the way.

"Oof!" I hit the ground as the energy whizzed by and fizzled out.

I realized that the person pinning me to the ground, shielding me with his own body, was my dad. "Are you all right?" he said.

Before I could answer, something like a battle cry echoed all around us, and the street erupted with pounding footsteps.

"The leprechauns!" Luken cried.

Sure enough, dozens of rainbow-colored beams shot through the air, aimed at the Queen Fairy. She waved off the energy beams like they were mosquitoes.

My dad pulled me to my feet. "Are you all right?" he asked again.

"I'm fine," I said, ushering him behind a nearby float for protection.

As the energy beams continued to fly, some of the fairies in the crowd jumped forward to defend the queen, but others joined the leprechauns in the fight. Alongside them were tons of creatures—including mermaids, pixies, and trolls—armed with everything from oysters to shoehorns. I saw Pryll leading the charge beside Karfum. The time for peaceful strikes was over. Finally, the creatures had found a way to work together, and they were determined to defeat the queen.

"What do we do?" I heard Mahlia cry.

"Nothing," said the queen, continuing to deflect the energy beams like they were spitballs. "Their magic will run out soon."

But she was wrong. As one line of fighters used up their magic ration, another line came forward to keep up the attack, while the creatures without magic helped in any way they could. There was no stopping them.

At Karfum's side, I spotted Belthum and three other young leprechauns fighting furiously. It looked like Karfum had finally managed to get his children back, and there was no way he was going to let anyone take them again.

As the charging crowd grew bigger and more determined, the Queen Fairy suddenly seemed terrified. Then an energy beam hit her right in the arm, setting her sleeve on fire. She howled and darted toward Mahlia.

Pop! The two of them disappeared.

"I need to go after the queen," I told my dad. "Stay here."

"No, we'll help you," my mom said, rushing to my side. At that moment, it didn't matter if my parents remembered me or not. All that mattered was that we were adventurers, and we had a job to do. Together.

As the three of us dashed down the street, I caught sight of Karfum and Luken shouting out orders as more of the queen's fairies tried to attack. I was glad to see that some of the fairies were putting down their weapons and surrendering to the leprechauns. It looked like they were sick of being prisoners in their own land.

After weaving around an abandoned pumpkin taxi, my parents and I finally got to the palace and charged inside.

"Where do we go?" my dad said.

"Top floor. The Queen Fairy's quarters," I said. "I don't know where else she would be." I led my parents to the elevator, but it didn't open. Either the magic knew not to let us inside, or there wasn't enough of it to run the palace anymore.

Great. Now what?

"Maybe we can climb up somehow?" my mom asked.

"The slides!" Luken had told me the slides in the palace usually ran alongside the elevator shafts. After I explained to my parents what to look for, we scoured the hallway for one of the hidden panels.

As my dad and I searched every inch of the wall, I couldn't help glancing over at him. Standing next to him was pretty much the best thing ever.

He must have seen me looking at him, because he gave me a little smile. "Once this is all over, we'll have to catch up," he said.

I nodded. Hopefully, reminding my parents of the life they'd left behind would help spark their memories. But I'd have to worry about that later. Right now all that mattered was—

"Found it!" my mom called.

We hurried over to where she was pointing to a nearly invisible button that was the exact color as the wall. When I pressed it, the panel swung open, revealing a slide very similar to the one Luken had shown me.

I peeked inside, trying to judge how far up it went. It curved almost right away, so that I couldn't see anything.

"It probably goes all the way to the top floor," I said. "Just like the other ones. But I have no idea how to do anything except slide down." I stuck my hand inside, hoping to feel some sort of magic whooshing past, but the air was still.

My Sort of Fairy Tale Ending

My parents smiled at each other like they had a private joke between them. It had been so long that I'd forgotten a lot about my parents, but I remembered that smile. It meant they had something good up their sleeves.

"We might have an idea," my dad said. He turned to my mom. "Hop in, and we'll try it out."

"No, wait," I said. "I want to go first."

I could tell they wanted to argue. Even if I was a stranger to them, they were still being protective and parental. I guess that was their nature. But I couldn't let anything happen to them. If anyone was going to get zapped by a crazy fairy, it would be me. I guess that was *my* nature.

Before they could object, I climbed into the slide. When I was crouched in the tight space, I nodded at my parents. "I'm ready."

My dad stepped forward. "This is always the first thing we try." He cleared his throat. "Top floor. Abracadabra!"

Before I could say "seriously?" I shot upward like a rocket. I zipped up the slide, twisting and turning all the way, my tail curling around my legs. Right as my stomach was about to revolt, I realized I had other problems. I was hurtling straight toward the top of the building, aimed right at the glass ceiling.

Chapter Twenty-Eight

Just when I was starting to think my head would crash through the glass—ouch!—the magic faded, and I stopped moving. I found myself standing on a tiny ledge right next to the panel door. I had to get out of the slide fast before my parents shot up after me.

After I shoved the panel open and climbed out into the hallway, I heard my mom let out a groan inside the slide.

I helped pull her to freedom right before my dad appeared. Both of them looked a little green. Apparently, being in a coma for seven years and then going on a bizarro water-park ride wasn't a great combination.

"How did you know the abracadabra thing would work?" I whispered.

My dad grinned. "It's like a default magical password. You'd be surprised how often it does the trick."

I shook my head in disbelief. Knowing that little tidbit

would have been amazingly helpful during my years as an adventurer. If only my parents had been around to teach me these things...

I pushed the thought out of my head. There'd be time to dwell on all that later. Right now, the only thing that mattered was getting us, and all the other prisoners, out of Fairy Land.

The tunnel had brought us right by the elevator, which meant the throne room was just around the corner. Luckily, the fairy guards I'd seen here last time were all gone, probably trying to get the whole rebellion under control.

As usual, I found myself about to confront a super villain without an actual plan. I glanced over at my parents, whose faces were slowly regaining their normal colors.

"Any idea how we take care of this fairy?" I said softly.

"We usually figure things out as we go," my dad said. Well, *that* certainly sounded familiar.

"Sometimes you just have to shoot from the hip," my mom added.

I blinked. "What does that mean?"

"It's just an old saying," she answered. "Maybe people don't use it anymore."

I couldn't help smiling. I might not have known what

the expression meant, but I had a feeling it was just like the cheesy sayings that were always popping out of my mouth. Even though my parents couldn't remember who I was, there was no doubt we were related.

"All right, let's go," I said, turning down the hallway. My parents followed behind me. When we got to the doorway, I scanned the throne room, looking for the Queen Fairy's telltale glow.

Nothing.

"Maybe she's not here," my dad said.

"She has to be," I said. "I don't know where else she'd go."

Just then, Mahlia emerged from behind one of the hanging tapestries. Her powdered hair was frizzy, her dress was torn, and for once she wasn't holding her star-shaped wand.

"You are too late," she said, actually sounding sorry about that fact. "There is no stopping the Queen Fairy. The last part of her plan is almost complete."

"The last part of her plan?" I repeated. The Queen Fairy wanted nothing more than to go after the Committee, but how could she do that when there was no one who would take her there?

I gasped as I realized that maybe that wasn't quite true.

"Quick," I told my parents, "we have to find Anthony!"

Before we could move, a blinding light flashed all around us. I whirled around to find the Queen Fairy standing beside Mahlia. Her glowing hand was wrapped around someone's arm. But it wasn't Anthony in her clutches. It was Dr. Bradley.

"No!" I cried. "Leave him alone."

"Silence!" the Queen Fairy said. She turned to Mahlia. "I expect order to be restored when I return." The queen flicked her wrist, and the cuff around Dr. Bradley's wrist disappeared. "Do not think you can defeat me with your weak magic, old man. Now, take me to the Committee."

"He's not taking you anywhere," I said.

"Jenny," Dr. Bradley said in a papery voice. "I'm so sorry. She will hurt you if I don't do what she says. I can't let anything happen to you." He was pale and clearly exhausted, and his extra leg seemed to be pulling him off-balance. I'd never seen him look so old.

"No, please," I said, but it was too late.

There was another flash, and Dr. Bradley and the Queen Fairy began to shimmer and fade. Without thinking, I leaped forward and grabbed on to the doctor's free arm. Instantly, I was sucked into a glittery vortex. And then, just

as quickly, we stopped spinning and solid ground materialized under our feet.

Sure enough, we were in the Committee's blindingly
white hall. The old women were seated at their table as
usual, looking at us with stunned expressions on their
identical faces.

Chapter Twenty-Nine

"What is the meaning of this?" the Committee members demanded in unison (which was how they always talked). "You are not welcome here."

"That is irrelevant," said the Queen Fairy, tossing Dr. Bradley aside. He stumbled forward and fell.

"Dr. Bradley!" I cried.

"I am all right, Jenny," he said as I helped him sit up. "Don't worry about me." The orange cuff was back around his wrist, which meant he couldn't magic his way to safety.

"Adventurer." The Queen Fairy glared down at me. "You continue to be a nuisance."

"Sorry about that," I said, straightening up. "To be fair, I think you're pretty annoying too."

"Leave this place!" the Committee members said as they got to their feet. I was surprised to see they actually had legs. I'd always suspected they might just be torsos attached to chairs.

"Not until I have what I came for," the Queen Fairy said, striding toward them. She'd only taken a few steps when the Committee members raised their arms and beams of energy shot out of their fingertips, all aimed right at the Queen Fairy.

The glowing fairy stumbled backward. For a second, she even looked like she might fall over. Then she righted herself and kept charging toward the Committee.

"Unacceptable!" the old women cried in outrage. They let loose a bigger wave of energy, and this time the Queen Fairy was thrown back like she'd been punched in the gut. She let out a hideous screech as she hit the tile floor.

"Leave this place!" the Committee members intoned again.

The Queen Fairy scrambled to her feet. The glow coming off her skin had dimmed a little. Maybe that meant the Committee really was stronger than she was.

Then the fairy's black eyes swung toward me. Before I could do anything, I felt myself being pulled toward her by the force of her magic. Then her long arm wrapped around me like an electric eel, almost burning my skin with her power.

She started to walk toward the Committee again, holding me in front of her like a shield.

"Do what I say," she hissed at the Committee, "or your precious adventurer dies."

I couldn't help letting out a honking laugh. "Yeah, right," I said. "Those old bats hate me. If you kill me, you'll be doing them a favor."

The Queen Fairy acted like she hadn't heard me. She just kept inching forward.

I expected the Committee members to simply roll their eyes and zap both me and the Queen Fairy without a second thought. So I was shocked to see them whispering among themselves, like they were actually considering what the Queen Fairy had said.

"Very well," they said finally. "Release the adventurer, and we will cooperate."

"You can't be serious!" I said, stunned. Since when did the Committee members care about me at all? Let alone enough to surrender themselves—and the magical kingdoms—to keep me safe?

"Release her," the old women said again.

Instead of letting me go, the fairy waved her hand and instantly, four identical orange cuffs appeared on the

Committee members' wrists. I was willing to bet those cuffs would suck up all the magic the old women possessed.

"Finally," the Queen Fairy said, as her skin started to glow more brightly than ever before. "I will no longer have to live in fear of you like my father did. Once I have conjured my prince, we will be the most respected rulers in the magical kingdoms, and no one will ever have power over the fairies again."

The Committee members stared down at their wrists in shock. I couldn't really blame them. They were used to controlling everything, to having the magical kingdoms under their identical thumbs. They'd probably never imagined that someone could enslave them, especially someone who was doing all of this to get a boyfriend.

"No!" I said. "Leave the Committee alone!"

I tried to fight out of the Queen Fairy's grip, but she shoved me toward the floor with all her strength. As I hit the tile—*crack!*—I heard my head make a sickening sound. Then everything went black.

• • •

When I opened my eyes, my head was pounding like someone had used it as a punching bag.

I tried to sit up, but everything was spinning around

me, and my body felt weak and shaky. I lay back down, the cool tile soothing my aching head.

Out of the corner of my eye I could see Dr. Bradley hunched on the floor nearby, motionless. In fact, he was so much like a statue that I realized the queen must have paralyzed him with her magic so he wouldn't interfere with her plan.

Her plan! I had to stop her from taking the Committee's magic!

I managed to move my head slightly and spotted the Queen Fairy hovering over the Committee members who were now slumped in their chairs, asleep. Keeping them unconscious probably meant she could soak up their magic even faster.

I hoped she sucked up so much power that it made her head explode.

Wait. Maybe that was the answer. Maybe there *was* a way to defeat her, after all.

I tried to sit up again, but I was still too weak and dizzy to move. My head felt like a hundred-pound weight someone had attached to my neck. It even hurt to think.

After struggling to move a few more times, I eased my pounding head back on the cold floor. It was no use. I couldn't do anything to make my plan work. All I could do was watch as the Committee's power was drained away.

My hope started to evaporate. Maybe this was really it. Maybe my days of saving the universe were finally over, and any chance I had of getting my family back was gone.

Chapter Thirty

Just when I was about to completely give up, there was a blinding flash all around me.

Out of the corner of my eye, I could see that a whole crowd had appeared: Anthony, my parents, Luken, and Karfum. And, wait, Mahlia? What was *she* doing here? Had she brought everyone else as prisoners?

"It's over, Your Shininess," Anthony called out. "Time to give it up."

The Queen Fairy smirked at him. "Nonsense. Mahlia, take care of them. I have more pressing things to do."

Mahlia didn't move. Instead, she held her ground beside Luken.

"What is this?" the Queen Fairy said. "Mahlia, I said take care of them."

"No," said Mahlia. "I believed you were the hope for our future and that you could keep our children safe. So

I stood by and did nothing when you enslaved the lepre-chauns and took most of the magic for yourself. I cannot stand by and do nothing now that I see how selfish you really are." She took a step forward, clearly gathering her courage. "And for the record, I have never liked *Cinderella*!"

The Queen Fairy let out something like a howl. "You are as much of a disgrace as that son of yours. Very well, then I will take care of all of you!" She flung her arms out, and a wave of energy rushed through the room, knocking everybody over.

Luken landed like a limp doll only a few feet away from me. I sighed with relief when I realized that he and the others were still breathing. They'd just been knocked out.

The Queen Fairy stormed back over to the Committee and continued whatever creepy method she had for put-ting people into comas. I hoped that meant she was too distracted to notice what I was about to do.

"Luken!" I whispered. "Luken, wake up!"

He didn't stir.

Great. I couldn't shout at him or the queen would know I was awake. But there had to be some way to get through to him.

"Luken," I tried again, a little louder. "I need your help!"

Still nothing.

Slowly, I forced my hand toward Luken's head. The concentration made my head pound even more, and my whole body was shaking with the effort, but I couldn't give up.

Finally, my hand was right next to Luken's long ear, but when I went to pinch his earlobe, I was still too far away. Now what?

Then I remembered my tail. Slowly, using every last ounce of energy, I eased my tail along the floor like a snake until it was right next to Luken's head. Then I made the end of my tail poke him right in the ear.

"Ouch!" he said, his eyes popping open.

"Shh. Don't move. Pretend like you're still unconscious." He did as I said and lay still. "Now listen," I went on, barely at a whisper. "I think I know how to stop the Queen Fairy, but you have to do what I say. Okay?"

He nodded slightly.

"The Committee members are all asleep. You need to get into their dreams and tell them to push all their magic into the queen, all at once."

Luken's eyes widened in horror. "If I do that, then…"

"I know how it sounds. But think about what she's done,

Luken. She erased everything your father worked so hard for. She made Belthum and Pryll and so many others into slaves. And that's exactly what she'll do to the other creatures in the magical kingdoms if she gets the Committee's power. This is our only chance to stop her. Please, help me."

Luken thought this over, and for a second it seemed like he might agree. Then he gave me a woeful look and a small shake of his head. Even though he obviously hated the Queen Fairy, maybe he didn't want to be the one responsible for destroying her. Especially not after his mother had loyally served the queen for years.

I wanted to cry. If Luken wouldn't help me, then this was all over.

Just then, a long, pale hand reached out and rested on Luken's arm. I could just make out Mahlia on the other side of him. She gave him an encouraging nod, and I could tell she was assuring him that it was all right, that this was something they could do together. After all this time of blindly protecting Luken, she was finally willing to work with him.

They both closed their eyes, and I watched—my breath frozen in my chest—as looks of deep concentration washed over their faces.

My Sort of Fairy Tale Ending

The Queen Fairy was pacing in front of the Committee's table now, probably urging the magic to flow into her even faster. Then she stopped and glared in my direction.

"You!" the Queen Fairy roared. "You are doing something to me. I can feel it." She started to storm toward me. "I am tired of you and your parents trying to get in my way. You are just as foolish and weak-minded as my father was. Now that I am in control, I will put an end to all adventurers. I will wipe you away like pieces of dust!"

She was nearly on top of me, spitting glowing fairy saliva at me. I didn't care. As long as she was distracted, as long as she didn't notice that her skin was getting brighter and brighter and brighter, she could say whatever she wanted.

Her shrill voice abruptly fell silent, and she looked down at herself. "What is this?" she whispered. "What is happening to me?"

Her skin was so bright, it resembled molten lava. She stumbled backward, clutching her stomach like she was about to be sick.

"More!" I cried at Luken.

"I cannot," he said with a gasp.

As the queen started to straighten up, I realized it wasn't

enough. We needed one last push of magic to put an end to her.

Wait. If the queen had been using adventurers to magnify magic, then maybe I could do it too. While the Queen Fairy staggered toward me again, I inched my aching body closer to Luken, and then I reached out and grabbed his hand. The minute our fingers touched, I could feel Luken and Mahlia's magic flowing through me. It wasn't a lot, but maybe it would be enough.

I closed my eyes and let the magic wash over me like a warm bath. Then I imagined taking that warmth and funneling it into a single stream, molding it until it was almost like a laser. Finally, all at once, I pushed it as hard as I could away from me. Directly at the queen.

"Stop!" she screamed. "No!"

But it was too late. I opened my eyes just in time to see her skin start to break open, like the magic couldn't stay trapped inside her for a second longer. She glowed brighter and brighter and brighter, until—

Kaboom!

The entire room filled with blindingly bright light. Then the light turned into what looked like melted gold, raining down from the ceiling.

My Sort of Fairy Tale Ending

Finally, where the Queen Fairy had been, there was just a shimmering puddle.

Chapter Thirty-One

As bits of blinding gold fell all around me, I closed my eyes to keep from seeing stars for the rest of my life.

"Jenny!" Luken cried from somewhere above me. "Jenny, the queen is gone. She is really gone!"

I opened my eyes, trying to smile, but I could still barely see straight. Was there something really wrong with me?

"What is the matter?" Luken said, his smile disappearing. "Are you hurt?"

"Get...get Anthony."

Luken nodded and ran off. Almost instantly, he came back with the gnome beside him.

"Jenny-girl, are you okay? What happened?" Anthony knelt over me, his face full of concern.

"My head," I managed to whisper as things started to go black again.

Anthony got to work right away. He yanked off the

fairy cuff—which was crumbling to dust on its own—and started working some healing magic on me. A minute later, Dr. Bradley joined in.

Karfum also rushed over and stuffed some shamrocks in my mouth. "These will do the trick," he insisted. I was so exhausted that I obediently swallowed them down.

A second later, whether it was from the magic or the shamrocks, I started to feel better.

"My parents!" I said, trying to sit up. "Are they—?"

"They're fine," said Dr. Bradley. "Take it easy, Jenny. You have quite a nasty bump on your head."

I didn't care about all that. I scanned the room. Nearby, Luken was standing with Mahlia at his side, her arm draped protectively around his shoulders. For the first time, they looked like they were really mother and son.

"Jenny?" Luken said, coming over to me. "Are you all right?"

"I'm great!" I cried. "The queen's gone. Luken, you did it. You defeated her!"

"We did it together," he said, giving his mother a smile. I couldn't believe the warmth flowing between them. Maybe the two of them could finally figure out a way to get along.

I spotted my parents stirring on the other side of the

room, waking up from being knocked out. "Help me up," I said to Anthony. "Please. I need to make sure my mom and dad are okay."

Anthony nodded and helped me get to my feet. I was still a little dizzy, but that didn't stop me. When I rushed over to my parents, my dad was looking up at me with puzzled eyes.

"Jenny, is that you?" He looked around. "What happened?"

"The Queen Fairy's gone," I said.

My mom sat up a few feet away, holding a hand up to her forehead like she had a headache. "How did we get here?" Her eyes went wide at the sight of me. "Jenny. It really is you, isn't it? You look so…grown up!"

I stared at her, afraid to ask the question. "You—you know who I am? You remember what I looked like when you left?"

My mother laughed. "Of course I do! Now help me up so I can hug you! Is that my necklace you're wearing? And my bracelet? Wait, am I seeing things, or do you have a tail?"

I couldn't believe it. My parents knew me! Their memories were back! I pulled my mom and dad into a giant hug, not wanting to let them go. This time I didn't cry. I just laughed and laughed, unable to believe that I had finally gotten my family back.

After a minute, Anthony and Dr. Bradley joined in our group hug so that we became more of a football huddle. I couldn't remember ever being so happy.

Finally, when we could all let go of each other, it was time to figure out how to fix the mess the Queen Fairy had left behind. Luckily, the cuffs on all of our wrists were falling off, and the last of our mousy features were disappearing. My tail was getting smaller by the minute.

"I will check on the Committee," Dr. Bradley said. He conjured himself a new cane before hobbling over to where the Committee members were starting to wake up. I wasn't sure where all the stolen magic had gone when the Queen Fairy had disintegrated, but I had a feeling it had returned to where it was supposed to be. Which meant...

"The Land of Tales!" I said. "We need to go there and make sure everyone's magic comes back. And Ilda, we need to figure out what to do with her. And my friends—"

"Jenny-girl, relax!" said Anthony. "You go rest up and be with your family. I'll take care of everything, and I'll bring Trish and Melissa home from the Land of Tales when they're ready."

I threw my arms around Anthony and held him tight. The last of my dizziness was gone. Now I just felt like my body was about to burst with joy. "Thank you!"

When the gnome was gone, I introduced Luken to my parents. I couldn't let go of their hands, at least not yet.

"Now what happens?" I asked him. I glanced over to where Mahlia and Karfum were talking softly with each other.

Luken sighed. "The leprechauns will have their pots of gold returned to them, and all the prisoners will be allowed to go home, though it may take a few days to sort them all out. I am afraid it will also take some time to make Fairy Land run without magic."

My mom gave him an encouraging smile. "Your world will be very different, but the Committee will help make it right again. We all will."

"What about the theme park?" I said.

"My mother and I will rebuild it together, using my father's designs." Luken smiled shyly. "And maybe a few of my own." He took his sketchbook out of his pocket and showed me a drawing he must have done earlier. It was of both of our families strapped into a Gravitron ride, all of us looking sick, terrified, and totally happy.

I laughed. "It's about time you guys did the

amusement-park thing again. It'll make all the tickets and screaming and stuff make a lot more sense."

"Thank you for your help, Jenny," he said. "You have your family back now. Enjoy your time together."

I grinned back at him. "You too."

I was actually tempted to hug him but was saved from embarrassing myself by the Committee members' demanding voices: "Adventurers! Come here, please."

The old crones were back to normal.

When my parents and I went up to the table, the women were perched there as if nothing had happened. Even their hair was perfectly in place.

"We are grateful to you," they said. Their eyes swung toward me. "Giving the Queen Fairy all of our magic was a risky plan. We are glad it worked. Otherwise—"

"Otherwise, you would've been really mad. I get it. Sorry. I couldn't think of anything else to do."

"No," they said. "You misunderstand. It was risky, but it was necessary. Nothing else would have been sufficient to defeat the Queen Fairy. We are proud of you, Jennifer. We want you to return to being an adventurer. We would be honored if you would accept."

I stared at them with my mouth hanging open. Had the

Committee members actually said they were proud of me? First they'd risked basically everything to save my life, and then they'd actually complimented me? Maybe there was more to these old women than I'd realized.

"Of course I'll go back to being an adventurer," I said. "It's what I do."

"Wait," my mom said. "Not so fast."

I frowned at her. "What do you mean?"

"I think we all need a vacation first," she said. "Some time as a family to get reacquainted."

"Yes," my dad added. "After that, we can talk about putting our lives at risk again."

I nodded. They were right. I had plenty of time to be an adventurer. Right now, the most important thing was making up for all those years I'd missed with my parents.

"Very well," the Committee members said. "Take all the time you need." I waited for them to demand that we sign some paperwork, or to at least stamp a form or two, but they just smiled at us in unison and waved us away. If this was what working with the Committee was going to be like from now on, I could certainly get used to it! Especially if I had my parents by my side.

I turned to my mom and dad. "Let's go home," I said.

Chapter Thirty-Two

Aunt Evie had to drink about a gallon of tea before she believed that my parents were really back. She just kept staring at them and gulping down cup after cup of Earl Grey. Finally, she plucked a tiny black kitten off her shoulder and ran over to hug us all. I'd never seen her really cry before.

"What happened?" she said. "Where have you been all these years?"

"It's a long story," my dad said. "Maybe we'll tell you another time."

"No," I cut in. "I think it's time Aunt Evie knew the truth…about everything. She's been so patient with me. It's not fair to keep her in the dark anymore."

My parents had some sort of silent conversation between them. Finally, they both nodded.

"Well, Sis," my dad said, leading Aunt Evie back to her

seat at the kitchen table. "You might want to prepare yourself for a pretty crazy story."

It took the three of us a while to explain things to my aunt, starting with the existence of the magical worlds, and then moving on to our secret adventurer identities. When I told her about everything that had happened to me while my parents had been gone, my mom and dad wiped tears from their eyes.

"I wish we could have been there with you," my mom said. "There's so much we wanted to teach you when the time came."

"It's okay," I said. "You're here now. And we've got plenty of time."

Then we told Aunt Evie about how my parents had given themselves up to the Queen Fairy seven years ago to keep me safe, and how we'd managed to finally defeat her today.

My aunt sat there petting the kitten the whole time, until it started to squirm in her lap. Finally, when we were done, she let out a soft laugh. Seeing its chance, the kitten quickly made a run for it and disappeared into the living room.

"That's a lot to take in," my aunt said. "And this is all

really true?" I realized she was asking me specifically. I guess after all these years of the two of us living together, I was the one she trusted the most.

"Yes, Aunt Evie," I said. "It's the truth. I'm sorry we lied to you. It'll never happen again. I promise."

"And you were really a mouse?"

I laughed. "Yup. It was the itchiest time of my life."

She nodded slowly. "All right." And that was it. No more explanation or convincing needed. I guess when you spent your life talking to animals, hearing about magical worlds and power-hungry fairies wasn't really that strange.

"So," my dad said. "What do we do now?"

"Well," I said, suddenly feeling shy. "There is one thing I've been dreaming of doing with you guys. If you're up for it…"

"Whatever you want," said my mom. "I think you've earned it."

The four of us hopped in my aunt's car and headed to a nearby mini-golf course to play together as a family for the first time ever.

Aunt Evie, of course, kept trying to hold her club upside down while a gecko perched on her head. My mom insisted on keeping score with a calculator, while my dad and I both practiced our swings in between turns, trying to outdo each other. During it all, the four of us were talking and laughing as if all that time we'd lost had never happened.

As my family and I played mini-golf with the sun setting in the background, I couldn't stop grinning. This was it. This was exactly what I'd been waiting for all these years. It might have sounded dumb to anyone else, but I couldn't imagine anything more perfect.

THE END

Acknowledgments

Here we are again. Normally, Jenny would roll her eyes at all this cheesy stuff, but she's feeling pretty grateful right now. In fact, we both are. So let's thank some people, shall we?

To Ray Brierly for reading more drafts of my books than anyone should ever be forced to (and for claiming to like each one).

To my family and friends for the endless hugs and support.

To my writing friends and online buddies, especially Megan Kudrolli, Alisa Libby, Heather Kelly, and Sarah Chessman.

To Ammi-Joan Paquette for believing in Jenny from the beginning.

To Aubrey Poole and the rest of the Sourcebooks team for making Jenny's (and my) journey an amazing one.

And to all the incredible UnFairy Tale readers out there who've made me feel like a real author.

About the Author

Born in Poland and raised in the United States, Anna Staniszewski grew up loving stories (especially fairy tales) in both Polish and English. After studying theater at Sarah Lawrence College, she attended the Center for the Study of Children's Literature at Simmons College. She

Sedman Photography

was named the 2006–2007 Writer-in-Residence at the Boston Public Library and a winner of the 2009 PEN New England Susan P. Bloom Discovery Award. Currently, Anna lives outside Boston with her husband and their adorably crazy dog, Emma. When she's not writing, Anna spends her time teaching, reading, and shooting hoops with leprechauns. You can visit her at www.annastan.com.

Be the first to discover Anna Staniszewski's brand-new series!

Wanted: Maid for the most popular kids in 8th grade.

Cleaning up after the in-crowd gets Rachel all the best dirt.

Rachel can't believe she has to give up her Saturdays to scrub other people's toilets. So. Gross. But she kinda, *sorta* stole $287.22 from her college fund that she's got to pay back ASAP or her mom will ground her for life. Which is even worse than working for her mom's new cleaning business. Maybe. After all, becoming a maid is definitely *not* going to help her already loserish reputation.

But Rachel picks up more than smelly socks on the job. As maid to some of the most popular kids in school, Rachel suddenly has all the dirt on the eighth-grade in-crowd. Her formerly boring diary is now filled with juicy secrets. And when her crush offers to pay her to spy on his girlfriend, Rachel has to decide if she's willing to get her hands dirty…

Read on for an excerpt from *The Dirt Diary*

"Rachel, what are you doing with that toilet brush?" Mom calls as she comes out of the house with a mountain of paper towels in her arms.

"Um, practicing?" I say, realizing I've been absently twirling the brush like a baton. I give it one more dramatic spin before chucking it into the back of our dented minivan. Really, I was distracted while calculating how much money I need to earn in the next month ($287.22) to keep from getting in huge trouble, but that is definitely *not* something I can admit to Mom.

"All right, are we ready for our first day?" she says as she slides the minivan door shut. She's grinning so widely that the skin by her ears is wrinkling.

I nod and try to smile back. I can't believe I actually volunteered to give up my Saturdays to inhale bleach, but my efforts will all be worth it in the end. Fingers, toes, and eyes crossed.

We pull out of the driveway and head toward one of the fancy housing developments across town. To stop my feet from nervously tapping in my sneakers, I focus on my baking plans for the weekend. My mission is to create the ultimate to-die-for brownie. If that doesn't get everyone's attention at the Spring Dance bake sale next month, nothing will.

"I'm so glad you changed your mind about working with me," Mom says, pushing her honey-colored bangs off her forehead. "It'll be nice to spend some time together again."

"Yeah, it'll be fun," I say, my voice high and squeaky. "I looove Windex!" I find myself doing what could be a cheerleading hand motion to show her just how excited I am.

Mom's eyebrows scrunch together, and I tell myself to calm down. Mom miraculously accepted that I'd suddenly changed my whole attitude about her new cleaning business in the span of two days. She *cannot* know the reason why.

"Just remember that we need to make a good impression today, so try to be friendly, all right?" she says, glancing over at me.

Something stabs at the pit of my stomach. "You mean, try to act normal."

Mom sighs. "Rachel, why do you have to be so down on yourself? You're going to be in high school next year. It's time to get some self-confidence." Mom has never had an awkward day in her life, so she thinks being freakishly shy is just something you can switch off like an infomercial.

"I *do* have confidence," I insist. At least, I do in my ability to make an amazing dessert. Dad always says my recipes are a little piece of heaven on a plate. I just hope heavenly is enough to get the most votes at the bake sale this year.

Thinking about Dad makes a familiar ache spread through my chest. Ever since he moved to Florida two months ago—right before Valentine's Day, no less—nothing has felt right. Even Mom, who usually tries to smile and plan her way through every crisis, has been acting totally weird for weeks. That's why I have to make my Get-My-Parents-Back-Together Plan work, even if it means scrubbing every toilet in town. Our family just doesn't make sense without Dad.

A few minutes later, Mom and I pull into a neighborhood of gigantic houses. All the lawns and bushes are blindingly green, even though it's only the end of April. For some reason, I imagine the neon grass tasting like kiwi. Would a kiwi brownie be too weird?

We stop in front of a stone monstrosity with two towers, one on each side of the house. I can almost imagine archers camped out in the towers, on the lookout for intruders. A tiny brook winds around the house and under a bridge at the end of the driveway. That's right: these people actually have a moat.

After I drag myself out of the car, Mom loads me up with some cleaning supplies. I glance down at the mop in my hands. "Mom?" I say, pointing to a label on the end of the handle with the word "mop" helpfully written across it. "Am I going to have to take away your label maker?"

I expect her to at least crack a smile the way she normally does when Dad pokes fun at her Type A personality, but she just grabs the rest of our things and locks the car. I guess now is not the time to bring up how crazy-face Mom has been getting since Dad left. At least she'll have other people's houses to psychotically organize from now on.

When we reach the carved wooden front door, I suddenly feel super self-conscious in my ratty jeans and faded sweatshirt.

"Holy fish tacos, Mom. How do you know these people again?"

"My boss is friends with Mr. Riley. They play golf together."

Wait, Riley? I spot a gold plate by the door with *The Riley Residence* carefully etched across it. My stomach goes cold.

"Do the Rileys have a daughter?" I whisper.

Mom's face lights up. "That's right! I forgot Briana was in your grade."

Oh. My. Goldfish. Briana Riley. I scanned Mom's list of cleaning clients before we left the house. How did I not notice Enemy #1's name on it? I have to get out of here. If Briana sees me like this, it'll be even worse than the Troy fiasco. That whole mess gave Briana enough ammo to use against me for *months*.

But before I can move, the door swings open and a guy about my age smiles back at us.

"Hi there!" Mom says in the chipper voice she uses to answer phones at the law office where she works. "I'm Amanda Lee, and this is my daughter, Rachel. We're here to make your house spotless!" She lets out a little laugh that sounds like a hysterical chipmunk.

I expect him to at least raise an eyebrow at the idea of Mom and me being related, since we look nothing alike, but he just says, "I'm Evan Riley. Come on in."

"Is your mother here?" Mom asks as she files into the

foyer. I scurry after her, keeping my eyes down. I just have to get in and out of here without making a fool of myself.

"I'm the only one home," says Evan. "But I think she left a list in the kitchen."

"Great! We'll start there," Mom chirps.

Holy fried onion rings. I can't believe I'm in Briana Riley's house! And this has to be her twin brother. I've heard he goes to a private school for geniuses. So far, he seems a million times nicer than his sister. No one's ever mentioned how cute he is.

The minute the thought goes through my head, my face ignites. Why can't I even think a guy is good-looking without getting embarrassed about it? Of course, Evan isn't as cute as Steve Mueller. No one is. Steve Mueller is the hottest guy in the eighth grade, probably in our whole town. Unfortunately, as of a couple months ago, he's also Briana Riley's boyfriend.

"Rachel, come on," Mom calls, already down the hall.

I realize I'm still standing in the foyer, staring at Evan with my mouth open and practically drooling on myself.

He looks back at me with an uncertain smile. I can't help noticing that his eyes are the same shade of green as his Celtics jersey. "Are you okay?" he asks.

I try to nod and move forward at the same time, but that just makes me lose my balance. I stumble forward and—

Crash!

The mop and broom fly out of my hands and land on the floor, followed by several bouncing rolls of paper towels.

"Booger crap!" I cry, stooping to gather everything up. *Wait, did I just say that out loud?*

"Here, let me help," says Evan. As he kneels beside me, I catch the scents of peppermint and laundry detergent. "Did you just say booger crap?" he adds.

I nod, mortified. Why do Dad's goofy swears always have to pop out of my mouth at the worst times?

But Evan laughs as he gets to his feet, his arms full of paper towels. "That's funny. I think I might have to use that sometime."

I try to say "okay," but for some reason it comes out in slow motion. "Ohhhhkaaay." This is even worse than the one time I tried to talk to Steve Mueller!

Evan just laughs again, in a way that makes me think he isn't laughing *at* me. He grabs one of the rolls of paper towels and balances it on top of his head as he walks alongside me. I can't help smiling.

When we get to the Rileys' kitchen, I almost drop

everything all over again. Every surface gleams like it's covered in nonstick cooking spray. If we had this kind of kitchen at home, I'd be able to bake all the time without Mom complaining that I'm taking up too much space. I mean, they actually have three ovens!

"Thank you, Evan," says Mom, rushing to take the cleaning supplies from him. "We don't want to be in your way, so just pretend we're not here."

He shrugs. "I'll be in my room if you need anything. Don't worry about cleaning in there today." Then he glances at me and flashes a crooked grin. "See you later, Booger Crap."

Great. Perfect. Just the kind of nickname you want a guy calling you.

Ten minutes on the job, and I've already made a total fool out of myself. At this rate I won't even survive until lunch.

Catch up on Jenny the Adventurer's escapades in the
first two books of the series!

You Know all those stories that claim fairies cry sparkle tears and elves travel by rainbow?

They're lies. All lies.

Jenny has spent the past three years as an official adventurer. She travels across enchanted kingdoms saving magical creatures and fighting horrible beasts that most of you think are only myths and legends. She's never had a social life. Here friends have all forgotten her. And let's not even talk about trying to do homework. So—she's done!! Jenny is ready to go back to being a normal girl. But then along comes "Prince Charming" asking for help, and, well, what's a girl supposed to do?

I know what you're thinking:
"Can she talk to animals?"

Yes, those chatty woodland creatures won't shut up. It's not as cute as you'd think.

Jenny has a new mission in the Land of Tales (the crazy place all fairy tales come from) to face off with an evil witch and complete Three Impossible Tasks. Easy, right?

And this time, the stakes are even higher. Jenny's parents disappeared in the Land of Tales, and she's certain that if she can save the kingdom, she'll be one step closer to finding her family.

Being an adventurer is no fairy tale, but this is one mission Jenny can't fail.